B . J . BARTLETT

Is a New School a New Chance

THE FIRST QUARTER

authorHOUSE®

AuthorHouse™
1663 Liberty Drive
Bloomington, IN 47403
www.authorhouse.com
Phone: 833-262-8899

Published by AuthorHouse 10/15/2020

ISBN: 978-1-6655-0464-5 (sc)
ISBN: 978-1-6655-0462-1 (hc)
ISBN: 978-1-6655-0463-8 (e)

Library of Congress Control Number: 2020920331

Print information available on the last page.

*Any people depicted in stock imagery provided by Getty Images are models,
and such images are being used for illustrative purposes only.
Certain stock imagery © Getty Images.*

This book is printed on acid-free paper.

*Because of the dynamic nature of the Internet, any web addresses or links contained in
this book may have changed since publication and may no longer be valid. The views
expressed in this work are solely those of the author and do not necessarily reflect the
views of the publisher, and the publisher hereby disclaims any responsibility for them.*

Chapter 1

The Move

Today I start my first day at a new place. There are multiple reasons for that, but the main one is my dad got a new job in a new town. Now we weren't in a rich city, but this new town was very different from my old city.

Well I told you one of the reasons I had moved, but there is another one. I will tell you later, but for now it will be a surprise.

I'm currently a junior. I have played all sports. I was okay in basketball and soccer. I was good at football and the best in baseball. I was the quarterback in football. I played every position in baseball, for my glove hand was the best. At this new school I would only try out for football and baseball.

I had a little sister of age seven. She was in second grade. She had me in a spot where I could not deny her anything. Her name was Olivia.

My mom and dad both lived with me, and as far as I could tell we're happy. I loved all of my family dearly. If someone tried to mess with them they would have to go through me.

Anyways, my mom was signing me into my new school. As she was doing that the principle was sizing me up. He could tell I played sports, so he said, "The football team is on the field for tryouts. I'm sure they would let you play."

I smiled and said, "Thank you sir. I will do just that if my mom here is okay with it."

My mom said, "Of course I'm okay with it. I always want you away from me. You pester me too much."

We all laughed before I hustled down towards the football field. When I got there I saw some cheerleaders practicing and the football team. Since I couldn't see the coach I looked lost.

A girl walked up to me and said "Are you a little lost?"

I laughed nervously, "Is it that easy to tell?"

"You look like you're new. And yeah it is that easy to tell. If you tell me what, or who you are looking for I can probably help. My name is Jasmine," the girl said, putting out her hand in greeting.

"Thank you Jasmine. My name is Jason. And I was looking for the football coach," I say, shaking her hand.

On a second look I could tell this girl was beautiful. She was five foot and two inches tall. She had some pretty blue eyes that had a little twinkle in them that made her look mischievous. She had long blonde hair that went down to her waist. I was actually surprised she wasn't practicing with the cheerleaders, for she had an athletic build to her.

I must have been staring pretty long, for she smiled and asked, "Like what you see?"

"Uh ...I'm sorry. Where was the coach again," I say nervous that I messed up a chance to make a friend.

I was no eyesore myself. I was six feet and two inches tall. I had about half of my neck length covered in dark brown hair with some slight curls. I also had blue eyes and the athlete build.

Jasmine laughed, "I'm just playing with you Jason. You know you aren't a bad guy compared to some of the jocks. The coach is over there. The one that is constantly looking back and forth from his notebook to his players." She pointed to the coach while she said it.

"Well it was nice meeting you Jasmine. Hopefully I will see you around," I say.

"So I can help you to your classes maybe," She smiles. And yes that was part of the reason, but there were also two other facts. One of them was that she was cute. The other was I actually wanted her to be my friend.

When she said that I ran over to the coach. "What do you want," the coach asked gruffly.

I put my hand out in greetings and say, "I'm Jason, and I would like a chance at playing quarterback this year.

The coach shakes my hand and says, "I'm coach Wade, and if you are even half as decent as you were last year I will gladly let you try out. Get out there and give me five laps. When that's done grab a ball and head over to the group over there on the left. They are our defense team, so we would like to give them a challenge. The coach over there is named coach Lane. If he has any problems tell him I sent you."

"Sir yes sir," I say as I run my laps. I finish the five laps in under twelve minutes. When I finish I go over to the defense team and talk to coach Lane.

"You any good kid," coach Lane asks in a joking voice. It doesn't surprise me that he knows I'm good, for I played his team a lot of times in the past.

I ran over to where the second and third stringers for offense are running plays and asked for the ball. The kids don't argue, but the quarterback doesn't look happy.

"Okay guys you may not trust me yet, but let's try a shotgun play. I want the wide receivers to give me post corner routes. Tight end I want you to run to the first down line, so we can get an easy first down just in case," I say in the huddle.

The coach waits for my nod that I'm ready and counts down, "1....2....3 go."

The ball is snapped back to me and I await for my team to get open. I see the tight end lose his defender so I pass him the ball. It was just in time, for someone came crashing down on me a second after I released the ball.

The pass was perfect. It hit the tight end on the run. He caught it and took off down the field. He made it to the defense's ten yard line before he got dropped.

Once back in the huddle the tight end said, "Great call. My name is Antwan by the way."

"Nice to meet you Antwan I"m Jason, and that was a nice catch, though I did expect you to be tackled before you got here," I said.

"Well you caught the defense slacking," one of the wide receivers said. "I'm Dave."

3

The other wide receiver said, "I'm Drake and let's catch them on their toes again."

I called a running play. The boys all agreed and I nodded my head signalling we were ready. The coach counted down again. The second he said go the ball was snapped back to me. I made it look like I handed it over to the halfback, but actually gave it to the full back. The full back ran beside the tight end and I followed a little behind and off to the left in case a lateral was needed.

The play worked and got us a touchdown. When we did another hour's worth of plays like that the coaches called out positions. They said I would be the starting quarterback, and the guy that was the starting quarterback gave me a glare as he got the position of backup quarterback.

When that was done all of the guys ran to the showers except for me, for I had not brought extra clothes because I didn't know tryouts would be today. I walked back towards the bleachers and sat down. Some of the cheerleaders walked over to me and I could tell they were going to start flirting. I was still polite and said "Hey ladies I'm Jason."

They introduced themselves as Haleigh, Kayla, Jennifer, Taylor, Christie, Alexis, and Abbie. Kayla was the head cheerleader and also the head flirter.

I didn't mind of course, but earlier this year I said I would focus on my work instead of girls. I only said that because I was hurting from a breakup, but I also really needed to.

I must have looked uncomfortable because a familiar voice said, "Why don't you stop Kayla. Can't you tell he is not in the mood for flirting?"

Kayla laughed, "And what are you going to do you wuss? You gonna kick a ball in my face, spike a ball in my face, or splash me. You are such a loser Jasmine."

That was what got me mad. The fact that someone talks down on another person always ticked me off. I'm sure that Jasmine was actually pretty cool too, so I probably made the biggest mistake. I jumped to my feet and said loudly, "Why don't you shut your mouth and leave."

Kayla snorted, "You got your own helper now Jasmine? Honey why would you waste your time on her when you could be with me." As she said the first part Jasmine flushed with embarrassment. The second part she said while practically rubbing herself on me.

"News flash Kayla. I don't like people who try to talk down to others. If I had to choose between you and Jasmine though it would be an easy option. Jasmine is way nicer than you," I said.

Kayla left in a fit followed by her pack of cheerleaders. "That probably was a bad decision, but thank you anyway," Jasmine said as she turned away.

"I'm sorry if I went too far Jasmine. I just hate people like her. They always think they're better than everyone else," I said.

Jasmine laughed, "You are not wrong, but I took you to be one of them. I mean you do play football."

"Well I was liked for how well I played, but before then in my old school no one would talk to me except the unpopular kids. And even when people would say hi to me I still sat with the unpopular kids," I said kind of trying not to embarrass myself.

"Well I'll catch you later Jason. I'm assuming that's you're mom over there waving at you," Jasmine said pointing to my mom.

"Yeah see you tomorrow," I said running up towards my mom.

When I got there my mom and Olivia were waiting for me. "Did you have fun Jwason," Olivia asked, mispronouncing my name like normal.

"Yeah. I think I made a few friends and I am the starting quarterback," I said getting down on my knees to grab her. "Did you meet any friends?"

She smiled, "Yes I made like a gazillion friends. I like my teachers too. Hopefully you didn't make any girl friends, for that would be icky. Boy's and girls can't be friends."

I laughed, "Well sorry, but I made one girl friend so far," I whispered in her ear "I also made one girl enemy too."

Olivia said, "Ohhhh. Tell me all about it."

I lifted her up and carried her to the car on my shoulders. "I'll tell you in the car, but you must behave later and brush your teeth before you go to bed. Deal?"

Olivia shouts, "Deal!"

Chapter 2

The First Day

I was just getting into my 1967 mustang ready to drive Olivia to school when I realized I had to buckle Olivia in. I got out and buckled her in. Normally I wouldn't forget, but I was anxious to go to school.

Late last night I had programmed my phone's GPS to the elementary school. I drove there last night to find out how long it would take to get there, and I was bored.

Now I drove there like I had been doing it for awhile. When I got to the school Olivia tried to go, but I stopped her. "There are two things you are forgetting. One is that you need to be safe and have fun," I said. "And you must get a kiss from me before you leave." When I said that Olivia started squirming around trying to escape. I grabbed her and kissed her on the forehead.

Olivia said, "Yuck." Then she kissed my cheek and left. As soon as she got in the school I left for my school. On the five minute drive I thought about all of the new kids I would meet and hoped I'd meet Jasmine.

When I got in the school I looked for someone I might have known. Someone called my name after a minute and I looked over and saw Kayla. She took my schedule and was surprised to see I had all high level classes. She thought I would have the same classes as her, for most football players did take easy classes, but I did football for fun, so I made my grades more important.

She looked shocked enough that I knew she didn't know where my classes were. I snatched my schedule back and headed back to the door. I saw Jasmine enter the door. I started to walk over to her when a group of people walked beside her. As I was looking through the crowd trying to find her Kayla grabbed me and turned me around.

Jasmine must have seen me, for she was on her way to me. She saw my discomfort instantly and shouted out, "Hey Jason what are you doing? I'm supposed to show you around."

I sighed, "Thanks for coming here. I could really use a guide for the day."

She grabbed my schedule and said, "The high classes, you had me fooled. I have the same first, second, fourth, and fifth block. Your third and sixth block are right on the way to mine, so I can show you where to go."

I smiled and gladly followed her away from a mad looking Kayla. When we got a few feet away I said, "Thanks for that save. I thought I was dead."

She smiled, "Well glad I could save you from the vultures. Mrs Lola is an amazing English teacher. I had her for two years already, but she and I joke a lot, so good luck learning."

I laughed, "Sounds like it might be fun. Do you have any sports interests?"

"Ah I wondered when you would get to the personal stuff. Yeah I play soccer, volleyball, and I'm also on the swim team," Jasmine said teasing me.

"Well now I know I have two sports to watch and one that I didn't know this school had. I would like to join the swim team as long as It's not an all girls team," I said.

Jasmine looked surprised. "You swim?"

"Yeah I also play baseball," I said trying to get her to learn some about me, so she would tell me stuff I could know about her. I was thinking this could be the start of a good friendship.

We reached the class before we could continue the talk and Jasmine said, "Good morning Mrs. Lola."

Mrs. Lola was about five foot and two inches tall. She looked up and said, "God I thought I got rid of you Jasmine. Don't let this nuisance fool you into believing she is my favorite." As she said that she was trying to hide a smile.

7

"I won't let that happen ma'am. I'm Jason and she is just my guide," I said. "She also can't be your favorite, for you just met me."

Jasmine played hurt while Mrs. Lola laughed. "I'm going to like this kid even more than I thought. You may sit wherever you like. Jasmine, are you planning on joining drama this year?"

"Of course. Your favorite student wouldn't dare miss your favorite activity," Jasmine replied.

"So I guess I'm joining then," I said causing Jasmine to glare at me.

"Looks like we will have a new actor this year," Mrs. Lola said smiling.

"No ma'am. I'd rather be doing the lights or backstage if you already have someone on the lights," I said, remembering doing the lights for last year's play.

"Seems you may be in luck. We have only me to work the lights, and I really only do it for the kids. If you have any sports that you play we will work around it," Mrs. Lola said.

"Thanks ma'am. I will love working with you in and out of class. Your favorite student can't let the want to be your favorite student surpass him," I say, causing Mrs Lola to laugh.

The class ended fast sadly, for I actually liked it. Jasmine was the but of many jokes told by Mrs. Lola. Well not just Mrs. Lola. I also said some and we all laughed like we had been friends for years.

The bell rang and Jasmine led me to history. "Mr. Wade is the teacher. He probably already likes you after seeing you practice yesterday."

"You were watching me practice," I ask, causing her to smack my arm.

"Come on now Jasmine, you know the rules. No hitting one of my players. Especially the one that will be winning us the football season," coach Wade said.

"I won't be the one to make you win. The players are only as good as the team sir," I replied honestly. Like I said earlier I don't like people who think they're better than everyone else.

The coach smiled. "So rare that a sports player is humble. I like that kid, but don't think I'll go easy on you in this class, or on the field," he said.

"Good, I like a challenge sir," I replied.

That class was okay. We did some fun stuff like a group project, but history was never my favorite class. I can't say I was glad when the bell rang, but I did like the fact that I was moving on to my next class. That class was P.E. I know it probably was pointless to take that class since I already worked out after school for sports, but sometimes I learn a new game I would like to play.

Jasmine was walking me to that class when one of her friends yelled, "Jasmine, wait up!" When she caught up she hugged Jasmine and asked, "Who is the new guy?"

Jasmine looked flustered, "Oh my god I'm sorry. This is Jason. Jason meet Kira. I have known her since the beginning of highschool."

I put my hand out, but Kira just hugged me. "Any friend of Jasmine gets a hug from me. Especially the cute ones," She said which caused me to blush.

Jasmine laughed and asked, "Do you have gym class KIra?" When Kira nodded her head Jasmine continued "Can you make sure this kid doesn't get lost, or dragged by Kayla?"

Kira laughed, "Are you already taking a claim on this kid?"

"No I just defended her from Kayla yesterday at tryouts, but only after she saved me from having to be snatched up by the girl," I said.

"Ohh I bet that made her mad. No guy ever refused her before," Kira said.

"Well she must really not like me now. I did it twice with Jasmine's help and once alone now," I said.

"A man with true taste. To bad Jas called dibs on you. Though I bet you'd make a great couple," Kira said.

I can not tell you whose face got redder out of me and Jasmine. What Kira said did strike a cord though. I did like Jasmine, but I did say I would not date anyone, for I don't want my past to repeat itself.

"Well hopefully now that I'm leaving, Kira will stop embarrassing me," Jasmine said as she kept walking while me and Kira walked through the gym doors.

"That will happen because of the fact I'd like to get to know you now that the nuisance is gone," Kira jokes.

I laugh "Well what do you want to know?

As Kira is about to reply, the old starting quarterback walked in the gym and sneered at me. "Look at this chump. He is already hanging with the nerd group. We got a loser on the team boys," he says to his pals on the football team.

My anger started to flare. Kira did have on a pair of glasses and she was smart from what I could tell, but that did not make her a nerd and no one had any reason to call her one.

"Why don't you get lost Matt before Jason takes your friends as easy as he took away your position," Kira said

Matt took a step closer and his posse followed. "What will you do about it nerd," he sneers. He was trying to slap her, but his hand never made it near her face.

In a deadly quiet voice I said, "I advise you to shut your mouth before I rip your arm off and beat you senseless with it." Fear flickers in his eyes before he realizes he has backup.

"You might want to rethink that. If you try my friends and I will tear you a new one," he says.

"By the time they take even another step you'd have no arm," I growl back.

Chapter 3

Another Enemy

"You wouldn't dare," Matt said back, but his eyes gave away the fact that he was scared.

"I would. If you were smart you'd stay away from Kira, me, and all of her friends. If you don't you will find out if I was lying or not," I replied.

At that moment a teacher yelled, "What in the world is going on here. I'm gone to help out the new teacher and a fight is about to start. Who started this nonsense?" Of course Matt and his group shout that I did while any of the kids Matt had picked on yelled that Matt did. I just sat there in silence and dropped Matt's arm out of my hand, for that is why his slap never connected.

"Sorry coach. Won't happen again," I call out.

"You the new kid? I was just helping your mom out with her classroom, so that must make you Mr. Wilson. I'm coach Johnson," the coach said. I forgot to mention that my mom taught art class at this school.

"Yes sir I'm Jason Wilson," I said walking over to him

We shook hands and under his breath the coach said, "What happened here?"

I follow his example and reply, "Matt tried to hit Kira. I stopped him and told him if he tried again I'd rip his arm off and beat him with it."

The coach smiled. "With a threat like that you must play sports. Also from your build it looks like you play multiple sports, so do you play baseball?"

"Yes sir. That is why I knew I could beat him senseless with his arm. Why did you ask if you don't mind explaining sir," I say. You may notice I don't call any adult by their name, but that is because I think it's more respectful to say ma'am or sir.

"I'm the baseball coach, and with the way you handled that, for I was watching the whole time, I want you on my team," coach Johnson said.

"I'd love to be on it sir," I say.

"Well stop lounging around and give me some laps," he yells at all of the kids.

I returned to Kira who asked, "Are you in trouble?"

"Nah he saw the whole thing, but he did ask me to join his baseball team," I replied as I started to run some laps. When we ran ten laps around the gym the coach told us to play. I grabbed a football and asked Kira if she wanted to play catch. She said yeah and asked two of her friends who also agreed.

Before we started Kira introduced the two of them. One of them was a boy and the other a girl. "Bryce is this big ox while Miley is this little toothpick. Guys this is Jason," Kira said. I shook hands with Bryce, but Miley hugged me.

Once we started throwing the ball back and forth me and Kira started talking since we were beside each other. "That was really nice what you did for me. I thought once I heard you were a football player you'd let him hit me, but I guess you are not like most jocks. No wonder why Jasmine likes you so much," Kira said.

I laughed, "Jasmine doesn't like me. Maybe as a friend, but not anymore than that."

Kira laughed, "I've been her friend forever. I can tell when she likes someone, but I also know she won't admit it to herself yet. So the million dollar question is do you like her?"

I stuttered, "Uh...i...it's only been a.......a day..um ...how would I know?"

Kira said, "Well looks like you both won't admit it. Describe her to me."

"She has long blonde hair. Blue eyes with a twinkle in them that definitely is mischievous. She is five feet and two inches tall. She has a nice laugh and the best smile," I say before my face turns red as I realize I just admitted I liked her without knowing.

Kira winked at me and said, "Don't worry your secret's safe with me."

"Well since you know that now is there any chance I could get with her maybe," I ask.

"There is no one holding her hand," Kira said.

"Well I hope this stays with us because I don't want a relationship now," I said as I chucked the ball at Bryce who caught it with one hand. I shout "Bryce why are you not playing football?"

"I play baseball and I don't want to play multiple sports. I can't work if I do. And I need all of the money I can get so me and Miley can go out as many times as we can."

"Oh you two are dating," I asked, caught off guard. I knew Bryce wasn't like a normal jock the second I met him. I also knew Miley wasn't a nerd. Still I was surprised, for they seemed like complete opposites.

The other three laughed which put me at ease. "You are not the first one who was surprised by us two. We are dating, so don't let this beautiful lady tell you different. It breaks my heart that she thinks I'm out of her league. She is truly out of my league," Bryce said passing the ball to Kira.

Gym class goes by real fast. The class alone made me three friends, but it also earned me the respect of a few others who had been targeted by Matt.

Yeah I made another enemy, but in honesty the look of respect and the friends it gained me was worth it. I know I probably shouldn't have threatened someone who had the whole football team on their side, but I'd see what happened next.

Since none of the friends I met in that class had Spanish three I walked up to coach Johnson. "Anything I could do for you Jason," the coach asked.

"Yes sir," I replied a little embarrassed. "Can you give me directions to spanish three with Ms Ragland?"

The coach chuckled, "No need to be embarrassed. Her class is down the hall on the right. You will see a staircase leading up. Take them and it's the first door on the left."

"Thank you sir," I said as I walked down the hall. I followed his directions and thankfully made it to the right class.

As I was entering the class Ms Ragland walked over and said, "I'm Ms Ragland."

I surprised her by saying, "Hola señora Ragland. Me llamo Jason. Me gusta la clase de español."

"Oh this class will be fun," Ms Ragland said. I nodded and walked to an empty seat. As I was sitting down I saw Jasmine walk in the class. I waved at her and she sat next to me before we could chat. The bell rang and Ms Ragland began a lecture.

When the bell rang ending the class Jasmine led me to the cafeteria for lunch. "How was third block," we both asked at the same time. We laughed and I said, "You first."

Jasmine said, "Art class was fun. Mrs Wilson was an amazing teacher. I would've rather have art with you instead though. My art class is during your gym class and my gym class is during your art class."

I hid a smile and said, "Did the new teacher like you."

Jasmine said, "Yea, or at least I think so." She turned and caught me smiling and failing to hide it. "What is so funny?"

I laughed and said, "I don't know, but there is a new teacher whom I asked you if she likes you. Now why would I care if some random teacher liked you?"

"Jason you're being a real...... Oh wait that was your mom. Duh," Jasmine said smacking her hand against her face.

I laughed then said, "Well my third block was eventful. I made three friends and also gained respect from others. Oh and if you see Matt walking around without an arm in a few days just know we never had this talk." I then explained the whole day right before we reached the cafeteria doors.

Jasmine laughed then said, "The line for lunch is there, but I brought my own lunch. If you'd like to sit with me I'll be out there." She pointed to a door that led to the football fields. Before I could ask why she ate out there, Jasmine ran out the door. I managed to see she had some blush on her face.

Now alone I walked to the lunch line and awaited my food. The lunch lady said, "You look new here, so I'll explain how this works. You can get a choice out of two meats or a salad, and two sides. You may also grab a fruit and any drink you want up there."

I smiled, "Thank you ma'am. May I have some chicken nuggets and fries please?"

The lunch lady laughs as she grabs my meal. She said, "At least some kids have manners here."

As I waited to pay for my lunch Kayla came up behind me. She tapped my shoulder and said, "Why don't you come sit with the cheerleaders and football players."

I laughed, "If I did that Matt would try to kill me. If I'm being honest though I'd never want to sit with you. Now if you'll excuse me I have to talk to this lovely lunch lady and pay for my food."

As soon as I said that I paid the lunch lady and thanked her for my meal. In the lunch line I left behind a very dumbfounded Kayla.

I walked out towards the stadium and started looking for Jasmine when I heard a male call my name. I cursed under my breath before I turned and saw Bryce and Miley walking towards me.

"Hey guys," I said. "Do you know where Jasmine sits?"

They laughed at my voice. I tried to sound normal and keep the blush out of my face, but I must have failed badly. Miley said, "We are heading there now. By the way, why did you turn down Kayla so fast."

"Let's just say she said some words that I didn't want to hear someone who has only been nice to me so far, so I just don't want to hang with her," I said.

Before we could say more on the subject Jasmine walked over and said, "Don't believe a word these two told you about me unless it was good things than you can."

"Of course. You only can be good. So they were all good things," I said. "Wait no you're the wrong person my bad. We only talked about the truth. So yeah we only talked about bad things."

Jasmine started to reply when she saw Miley and Bryce laughing. "Wow Jasmine. I never took you as one who believes a word jokers said," Miley said through giggles.

Jasmine smiled, "Oh I thought maybe these two were trying to make me look bad."

"And you care why? After that encounter yesterday you should know

15

I only judge people by the way they act. I don't care if everybody told me bad things about you. I'd still talk to you to find out how you really were," I said. As it processed through my head what I said a blush crept into my cheeks.

Kira appeared at that moment and said, "If you embarrass Jason again Jasmine I'll tell him some stories about you."

Everyone but me laughed as a blush crept into Jasmine's face. Bryce said, "Well at least there's even now. Can we show the jock that's not a jock his seat now?"

Chapter 4

Lunch Bunch

Once I was seated on the bleachers a couple of girls walked towards us. At first I thought they were a part of this group, but once the others saw them I heard some cursing. When they got closer I recognized some as the cheerleaders I met yesterday.

"Need anything ladies," a deep voice said. The voice came from a scrawny male who was about five feet and eight inches tall. The guy had on a pair of glasses and a smile.

"Not from a nerd," Abbie sneered. "Especially not a nerd who is a friend of these losers. We came for the new kid. We want him to…"

I interrupted her, "Well you must be either deaf or daft then. As I told your friend yesterday I want no part of people who think they are better than others, so unless you have a legit reason to be over here I advise you to leave."

Some of the other cheerleaders laughed with my group. Abbie stomped off after saying, "This isn't over."

"I wish it was, but buh-bye and good riddance," I yelled at her. When I realized two of the girls had stayed I said, "If you ladies are here to bring me in with the others you're wasting your time."

Taylor shook her head and said, "No we wanted to congratulate you for becoming a quarterback, but now it also looks like we should thank you for saying that to Abbie. She has been being mean to Kyle for no reason. I was actually about to tell her off then, but you beat me to it."

I asked, "Who's Kyle?"

Christie said, "Kyle is the guy that asked if we needed any help."

"Oh well he seems nice," I said. I turned to Jasmine and said "Does he normally sit with you guys?"

Jasmine nodded and said, "Us unpopulars stick together."

I looked around the stadium and asked, "Anyone see where he went?"

As I was saying that Taylor walked around the side of the bleachers. When she came back Kyle was with her. What I'm sure surprised all there was Taylor had Kyle's hand in hers. "Well looks like there may be even more new people sitting here today other than you," Jasmine said.

"Is that okay? If not I could leave," I whispered back.

"And leave you at Kayla and Abbie's mercy? I'm not that heartless," Jasmine laughed back. Then she said loud enough for the girls to hear, "You guys can sit with us if you want."

Before Kyle sat I stood up and offered my hand. "I'm Jason and it's nice to meet you Kyle," I said.

"It's nice to meet you Jason," Kyle said, shaking my hand. "Welcome to the lunch bunch."

I was surprised when I saw that Taylor and Christie were the exact opposite of normal cheerleaders. They were nice and had manners instead of the normal prissy bunch.

As everyone sat down I heard Kyle tell Bryce, "I'll give you two nuggets for the fruit cup."

Bryce replied, "Make it three."

Quietly I asked Jasmine, "What is going on."

Jasmine replied in the same manner, "They are trading their lunches. Basically it's a way to get a bigger amount of a certain item. Bryce always trades for the meat and Kyle always trades for the fruit. Sometimes we all participate, but it depends on what lunch is for the day. Even though I pack my lunch I can trade with them."

"So it's all in good fun and the trades can be refused," I whispered back.

"Yes they can be," Jasmine said. "Are you thinking about joining in?"

I nodded then said, "Kyle I'll trade you my fruit cup for five fries and Bryce I'll trade you two nuggets for five fries."

They both agreed and all watching laughed. I joined in, for I knew what caused it. Bryce didn't however, so he asked, "What is so funny."

Miley said, "He just made the same trade that you just refused by giving you two nuggets and Kyle a fruit cup. When he did that he also made it so the two nuggets were worth the same price as the fruit cup therefore causing you to reconsider the trade subconsciously."

Bryce looked at me with fake hurt. I laughed and said, "I would have worked if you would have not said anything."

Bryce said, "How could you be nicer to Kyle. You met me in gym. I thought we had a bond."

"We may have, but I know a person who makes bad deals and when I see one I love to ruin their deals," I said.

"So why did you only trade for five fries? Also it was a good deal for me," Bryce fake pouted.

"In my honest opinion five fries were way better than both the chicken and fruit," I said as I swiped a fry from Bryce's tray.

"Hey," Bryce yelled. "My fry. That's my fry."

The group was laughing and was distracted by Bryce's fake pouting, so I swiped a fry from Jasmine's lunch. After I grabbed it I saw Bryce grinning and knew I messed up. I mouthed *Don't say anything*, but I knew he would.

"Hey Jasmine, the new boy swiped a fry from you," Kyle said. I'm not sure who gave the worst glare out of me, Bryce, and Jasmine. Me and Bryce were glaring at Kyle for different reasons, while Jasmine glared at me. Finally I withered under her gaze and passed her another fry.

"I'll get you back Jason," Jasmine said. While she was distracted by me I slightly nodded my head and Bryce and Kyle both snatched a fry from her. Jasmine caught Kyle in the act and Kyle quickly gave her the fry back. She then saw Bryce toss a fry in his mouth and realized what happened. She gave Bryce puppy dog eyes and Bryce turned away.

"Can someone tell me when she stopped," Bryce said.

Miley laughed out, "Last time she did that Bryce got her a brownie sundae. Actually he got her three."

I quickly made for another fry on Jasmine's lunch tray. I got it and made sure Jasmine knew I had it. I then tossed it in my mouth and chewed. Once I knew her puppy dog eyes were on me I said "Bryce your good. She is now giving me the puppy dog eyes." I then turned back to her and pointed at my tray. I said, "I have no more fries, only a nugget."

She made her look sadder and I sighed. I grabbed the nugget and held it up to her lips. She quickly ate it and the others laughed. "I could have used you a while ago," Bryce said thankfully.

"I don't regret it. A fry is always the better meal choice," I said and Jasmine shook her head.

"So you aren't always right. Everyone knows that a chicken nugget is better than a fry," Jasmine replied.

"Well if that's the case," I said slowly reaching for her fries.

She slapped my hand then put a protective arm around her fries. "My fries," she said.

Chapter 5

The Rest of School

The bell rang and ended lunch. After dumping my tray I joined Jasmine and we walked down the hall. She led me to Precalculus and Biology. Since I wasn't sure what I wanted to do in life I decided the extra Math and science would help. I was glad that the class was a half and half class, for it allowed me to be in art class. As we walked in and took our seats the bell rang.

The teacher walked up to the front of the classroom and said, "Hello everyone my name is Mrs Lane. I will be both your math and science teacher. We will have fun in this class. There will be extra credit for the science class if you go to the science related events in town. There will always be handouts on my desk if anyone would like to know what and where those events are."

After that she began teaching math and science the class went by very fast and before I knew it I was getting up to leave. As I was walking out the door I grabbed a handout and saw that the next activity was on a Friday. The activity was just to go stargazing basically, but the people that would be there would explain everything that was seen.

I asked, "Hey Jasmine do you know where the Nightfall park is?"

"Yes I do," She replied. "Would you like me to bring you there for the extra credit?"

"That would be nice if it's not a bother to you," I said.

Before we could talk anymore I caught sight of my mom in the hallway. "Hey mom," I called out.

"Hey Jason and Jasmine," My mom said smiling. "Are you showing him around Jasmine?"

"Yes ma'am," Jasmine replied. She said catch you later to me and walked to the gym.

"She's a nice girl," my mom said.

I laughed and replied, "She is, but don't think she is changing my mind about dating. At least not yet."

My mom frowned, "Okay. By the way, don't think I won't fail my own son."

"I plan on doing my work," I said back.

Miley and Kira arrived at that moment and said, "Hey Jason."

"Hey Kira and Miley. This is my mom, but to everyone in the class including me it's Mrs Wilson. Mom, these are some of my friends. That's Kira and that's Miley," I said pointing them out as I said their name.

"Well welcome to art class kids," my mom said.

We walked in the class and sat at a table. Kyle walked through the door and looked around for a seat. I called his name and pointed to the seat beside mine.

"Thanks for that," Kyle said as he sat down

"Anytime," I replied. "So are you and Taylor dating?"

Kyle smiled and a blush crept into his cheeks. Miley giggled and Kira said, "That's a good answer."

"Okay guys let's stop picking on Kyle before my mom says something that makes me go redder than Kyle," I said, trying to get his back. It was a mistake because my mom was walking behind me as I said it.

"Would you guys like to see baby pictures of Jason, or maybe a video of him in the spelling bee," my mom asked.

I yelled, "Mom!" All of a sudden my face went from tan to the red of a tomato as my mom pulled her phone out.

"Were good Mrs Wilson. We will later though, but I'm afraid if he sees us watching he'd burst," Miley said and the others nodded.

When my mom left I slid in some headphones and started to work on our first grade. We were supposed to draw anything we wanted. I was an okay artist in my opinion, but a lot of people told me I was a great one. I was thinking about what I wanted to draw when an image popped in my head. I drew that image until about ten minutes before class would end. At that point I quickly drew a dog in a field of flowers.

Before my mom could collect my papers I slipped the first one in my bag. That photo was private. It was a picture of Jasmine as I saw her smiling. I was not ready to let my mom see how Jasmine was affecting me and I also wasn't going to turn it in until it was finished.

When my mom came over to my table to collect papers she saw I only drew a bit. "Everything okay Jason? You normally draw more than one thing in class," my mom said.

"Yeah. I just messed up many times on the dog. I couldn't decide which one I wanted to draw," I lied.

Before she could quiz me again the bell rang. "Do you still want to pick Olivia up? I could grab her. She's not that big of a nuisance," I said

My mom said, "What about practice?"

"It doesn't start for another thirty minutes. I could pick her up and bring her here so you don't have to stay late," I said.

"That would be nice," She replied.

I left and jogged to my car. When I got to the area I could see my car I cursed. Kayla and Abbie were sitting on my car. "Hey Jason," they said in unison.

I replied dryly, "Hey girls. Can you please get off my car? I have to go. Also how did you know this was my car and that I'd be using it now?"

"All of the football players go out before the practice begins. And this car is new, so we guessed it was your's. We need to talk though," Kayla said.

"Maybe later this is important. I need to get my sister from school," I replied.

"She can wait. We need to tell you about your new friends," Abbie said.

I yelled, "Get off my car!"

At that moment Jasmine approached, "Hey Jason am I still showing you where the elementary school is."

I thanked the lord and said, "Yes you are as soon as these girls leave. And if they don't leave soon I'll just drive with them on the car."

Jasmine smiled at that thought as the girls got off my car fast. As soon as they were of it I opened Jasmine's door and closed it once she got in. I ran to the driver side and screeched out of the parking lot.

"Wow this is a nice car," Jasmine said.

"Yeah. I love this beast. Thanks by the way for saving me again," I replied gratefully.

"It was no problem," she said.

I asked, "By the way how'd you know where I was going?"

"Kira told me when she heard you and your mom talk. She said she was afraid you might run into problems with those two, so I got there as fast as I could. I was staying back anyway because I was going to watch practice. You know to support both Bryce and you," Jasmine said.

"Would you like a ride home?" I asked hopefully.

Jasmine smiled "My mom was going to pick me up afterwards, but that would be out of her way, so if you're sure I would be glad for a ride."

"Okay call your mom and tell her you got a ride home," I said as I pulled out my phone and an aux cord. I hooked my phone up to the aux cord and asked, "What type of music do you like?"

"I like anything really. My favorite is hip hop,``she replied. I clicked on my normal playlist filled with songs that were by Bruno Mars, Ed Sheeran, Charlie Puth, Ne-yo, and some other great hip hop artists. The first song that played was *Lighters* by Bruno Mars, Eminem and Royce da 59.

I was surprised when Jasmine started to sing to it. In disbelief I asked, "You know this song?"

Jasmine nodded and said, "This is one of my favorites. It is one of the best ones Bruno Mars ever made after *Just the Way You Are.*"

I laughed, "That's my favorite by him too."

We enjoyed the rest of the car ride to the elementary school. We sang many of the songs that were played and chatted through others. When we reached the school an over eager Olivia ran to the car. I got out and picked her up. I kissed her on the cheek and said "Hey Olivia. Remember how I told you about Jasmine yesterday? Well this is her.

Olivia got out of my arms and ran to Jasmine. She said, "Hey Jwasmine."

Jasmine laughed and much to Olivia's delight picked up Olivia spinning her in a circle. She said, "Hey Olivia."

Once Jasmine put her down I buckled Olivia in. "Now who's hungry?" I asked.

"Me. I'm hungry," Olivia said in a precious voice.

Jasmine laughed out, "Me too."

I said, "Me three. Now Jasmine May you please tell me where the nearest fast food place is?"

As Jasmine directed me to a restaurant called Jacked Fries, Olivia asked her loads of questions. Finally I said, "Olivia if you don't slow down the questions I won't get you any dessert."

After that Olivia only asked a few questions and Jasmine said, "Thank you. It's fun to talk with her, but she talks really fast."

I laughed and said, "Yeah. She can be a handful, but I love her anyway. Right Livvie."

Olivia said, "Yeah Jwason. I love you too."

As she finished saying that Jacked Fries came into view. I parked my car and we went in. I got two cheeseburgers, a large fries, and a sprite. Jasmine got a cheeseburger and a large fries. Olivia got apple slices, a small fries, and some chicken nuggets. I also ordered two medium sundaes and a small one. The girls picked their flavor and I paid for the meal before Jasmine could get her wallet.

"I'm paying and that's final. I'm paying for three reasons. One you saved me from those devils. Two you were nice to Livvie. Three you showed us here. Oh there's a fourth one which is for being a friend to me. I always pay for my friends," I said as Jasmine was beginning to argue.

She just shook her head and said, "Fine."

When we sat down to enjoy our meal Olivia tried to first eat her sundae. I said, "No dessert until you eat your nuggets."

I finished my meal fast and started to eat my small sundae. I got a small because I knew I was about to practice, and too much food in your stomach is not good for practice.

We finished the meal in less than fifteen minutes and were at the school with five minutes to spare. My mom was waiting for Olivia when I pulled in and grabbed her as I yelled, "See ya later." I rushed to the locker room and switched to my football gear.

I was on the field before anyone else so I ran laps. I always did that if I was the first on the field, so I could build up on my cardio.

25

A few minutes later a few people in their gear ran to the center of the field. I recognized Antwan in the group who called my name. As I turned to see him Matt walked out. He sneered, "Looky looky at the man who was slower than a turtle. I could jog and beet you in a race."

Antwan shouted for him to knock it off, but of course Matt didn't. He continued yelling insults, so I jogged over. "Stop wasting your breath and race me then," I said.

"Gladly," he said.

Antwan said, "Three…..Two…..One…...Go."

The race began and I was falling behind, yet I still kept jogging at a slow speed. Matt was maybe on the second lap while I was at the end of the first one. Matt yelled, "I thought you said race."

I stopped after the second lap and waited for him to get to the third lap and then ran as fast as I could. Matt was fifty five meters from the finish line when I passed him the first time. He was ten meters away when I passed him the second time. He was so shocked he couldn't say anything. "Thanks for the race. It was nice to get a challenge." I ran two hundred meters in the time he ran ninety.

Matt said, "Impossible you must have cheated."

The observers said, "We watched the whole thing. Jason dusted you. That will hopefully teach you a lesson."

Antwan clapped me on the back and led me to the defense practice area, for the coach wanted his best quarterback to play against the defense.

As Antwan was telling the guys what just happened I went to coach Lane. "Sorry sir. I didn't know where the practice was so I ran some laps and got in a race with Matt."

Coach Lane said, "You didn't hear this from me, but I hope that you beat him."

"While I go run those five laps the boys just ran. I'm sure one of them will tell you," I yelled over my shoulder as I raced off.

Like I guessed one of the players told the coach as I was running. At first the coach didn't believe it, but as he watched me run he saw that I was already on my third lap in under five minutes.

When I finished my laps the coach had me and Antwan throw back and forth to each other. We didn't do any real game-like practices. The coach wanted us just to get used to the game again, but he said next week we would be playing again.

Chapter 6

The Drop Off

At the end of practice I walked towards the bleachers and yelled for Jasmine. Jasmine came down and said "Good practice. You can take a shower if you want. My parents wouldn't mind me being a little late."

I shook my head and said, "I shower when I get home, for my shower is a lot better and it also has a better temperature range."

"That was a nice race you had with Matt. I just hope you're that fast at swimming," Jasmine said.

"I'm just a tiny bit slower in swimming, but I still won't lose to you," I said smiling.

Jasmine hit my arm and said, "We'll just see about that Jason."

As we got to the car I went to Jasmine's side and grabbed the door for her. "Why thank you kind sir. I thought chivalry was dead," Jasmine said.

I replied, "I guess I didn't get the memo."

I closed her door and jogged over to my side and hopped in. Before I could drive off, Antwan walked over. I rolled my window down and said, "What's up."

Antwan asked, "Can I get a ride?"

I nodded my head and he got in the back. "What happened to your ride?" I asked.

"They got stuck at work for another hour, so they told me they couldn't pick me up." Antwan said.

"If you want from now on I can drive you home," I said.

"Thanks man. You want to take a right up ahead," Antwan said.

"So Antwan, why are you second string? I've seen you and the starter tight end play. You have caught more passes than him," I asked him.

"Well I've caught all of the passes cause you threw them. Scott has to catch Matt's passes and they are horrible. We do get changed, but I think since Matt and him are so close Matt's dad threatens the coach to keep him in. I'm surprised you're still starting," Antwan said.

"I probably won't be in a few days. Speaking of then What is the point of this scrimmage? I mean second stringers on offense on a team with the starting defense versus the starting offense and second stringers defense. I'm glad we won't have all second stringers, but wouldn't it make sense?" I quizzed as I pulled into his driveway.

"It would, but They want the best defense to play against the best offense to improve each other. Alright man I'll catch you later. Just don't forget anyone is allowed in for free," he said as he got out of the car.

"Now I believe I need to get someone else home, so where do you live?" I asked Jasmine.

She pointed to the right and said, "I live close to the park you wanted to go to."

"Well no wonder why you're willing to show me where the park is. How are you doing," I said as I rehooked up the aux cord.

"I'm doing great. You?," she replied back.

"I'm doing great, but just a tiny bit sore. I haven't ran that fast in a long time. It was worth it though," I said while clicking on a shuffled playlist. *Perfect* by Ed Sheeran played. I had to agree that this was perfect.

Jasmine sang the chorus then said, "Yeah it was nice to watch that. He was always cocky."

I sarcastically said, "I would have never guessed." Jasmine laughed and I became serious. I said, "I hope he learned a lesson. It would do him good not to be that cocky."

Jasmine grew serious and said, "I doubt it will. His dad owns the local car dealership. Anytime Matt doesn't get what he wants his dad makes the person preventing Matt from getting it to pay early. He's spoiled."

I nodded and started to think about that. "Did you get a car from there?" I asked.

"Yes I did, but Matt wouldn't want me. He wants the girls you've been blowing off," she replied.

I didn't say it aloud, but I thought Matt might try to make her become his girlfriend just to piss me off. I knew that would be the only way she would date that fool, for she seemed disgusted by him.

The only noise on the rest of the ride was the music. I was actually not even listening to it though. My thoughts were flying around in my head. I almost missed Jasmine's turn.

When I pulled in her driveway her parents walked out. "Hey Jasmine. Who is this?" her dad asked.

"Mom and dad, this is Jason. Jason this is my mom and dad, but to you it's going to be Mr and Mrs Kibbler. Don't worry they won't bite," she said that last part so only I could hear it.

"It's nice to meet you sir and ma'am," I said as I shook their hands.

"Wow since when did teenagers have manners," Mr Kibbler jokes.

"I think it's nice to see one that has manners," Mrs Kibbler adds in.

"Well my mom always taught me that manners was the way to win over anyone," I said.

Mr Kibbler said, "So are you using manners with Jasmine?"

Jasmine hit him as I said, "Yes sir. I'm really trying to win her over, but it's like running into a wall. She sure can be stubborn."

It was my turn for Jasmine to hit me, but before she could I grabbed her hand. "Not fair," Jasmine pouted.

"Play nice and I'll let go. I swear my seven year old sister is easier to handle than you," I say causing her parents to laugh

Jasmine kicked my shin and I let her go. She then slapped me and was about to do it again when Mrs Kibbler said, "That's enough Jasmine. Jason needs to be able to move tomorrow. Jason would you like a drink?"

I replied, "No ma'am. I must get home."

Jasmine's parents waved as I walked to my car. Jasmine followed, but I didn't notice. When I sat in my car Jasmine said, "Well looks like I won't be riding in this beast for a bit."

I laughed. "This beautiful artwork is no beast. She may be fast, but only if you have a lead foot. But anytime you want to you can ride in this," I said.

Jasmine smiled, "I'll hold you to that Jason. Drive safe Mr lead foot."

"I am always safe," I replied as I drove out of the driveway.

I was about five miles from my house when a car came out of a trail and hit me. The car hit right into my seat. My head swung forward and hit the dashboard. I probably would have screamed had I still been awake.

"Scott, that was good driving. The money drop off location is in that spot where we drank last night. The coordinates are on your phone's GPS," Matt said.

"I'll see you later Matt," Scott replied as he walked away from the stolen car. He stole that car just to hit me, but not one person would know that."

Chapter 7

The Recovery

I awoke in the hospital and saw Kyle beside me. I tried to talk, but my throat was dry, so I pointed to a bottle of water. Kyle passed it to me and I quickly drank it. "What happened?" I asked.

"You were in an accident involving a stolen car. You smacked your head on the dashboard and were laying there when I found you. I brought you to the hospital. I couldn't call your parents because I didn't know their number, but the whole lunch group knows what happened," Kyle said.

"Can you call my mom and tell her I'm here?" I asked him. When he nodded I gave him the number and a cop walked in.

The cop asked, "Do you remember what happened?"

I nodded and said, "A car ran headlong into me. From the speed it was going it must have been waiting for me. It went at most twenty miles per hour. I was going sixty and I guess the impact caused me to slam my head into the dash."

"Well I hope you feel better and we will find out who caused this accident," the cop said.

As he was leaving Jasmine ran through the door. She said, "Are you okay."

I started to nod, but pain instantly flared through my head. "I was," I said through gritted teeth.

"What did I tell you about driving safely," Jasmine said.

"Wasn't my fault," I muttered.

The doctor walked in and said, "Jason you should be fine, but try to get some rest tomorrow. Don't go to school. I have already informed the school you won't be there tomorrow."

"Yes doc," I replied. I was upset about that. I was even more upset about the damage to my car. It would cost five grand just to fix it. I had that much money, but it was all I had. I knew no matter what the cops said they wouldn't find out who drove the other car. I had a few guesses, but I had no proof.

"Your parents are on the way," Kyle said as he entered the room.

"Thanks Kyle," I replied.

"No problem man. You had my back earlier and I got yours now," Kyle said. After that he left and it was just me and Jasmine in the room.

"Hey Jasmine who is Matt's closest friend?" I asked.

"Scott. Why?" she replied.

I waited a second then said, "I think he was the one who did this. I have no proof, but I know Matt wants me out of the season and the cop said the car was stolen. My guess is Scott "stole" the car from Matt's dad and did Matt's dirty work."

Jasmine said, "That does sound like them, but there is only one way to tell." She grabbed her phone and texted Kira.

"What are you doing?" I asked.

Jasmine said, "Kira lives close to where Matt and Scott drank last night. Anytime Matt has Scott do something dirty for him he drops off money at the last spot they drank at. If it was Matt the money would be there. If the money is there Matt is going to be wishing he had Scott hit him with the car instead."

I smiled, "Wow, you really know how to make a guy feel better. Just do me a favor and stay away from him."

Jasmine grabbed my hand and I squeezed hers. She said, "I can't make that promise."

She waited with me there until my parents got there. "Hey Jasmine. Why are you here?" My mom asked.

"I decided to wait for you two to get here so he wasn't alone Ms Wilson," Jasmine said.

"Well that's very nice of you Jasmine," My dad said.

I looked around for Olivia and realized she wasn't there. I asked, "Where is Livie at?"

"She's at home. As soon as we got the call we had a babysitter to watch her and drove here. We didn't want her to see you if you were worse. We only knew you were in an accident, but it looks like you're okay," my mom said.

"Yeah. The doctor just told me to not go to school tomorrow. He said he had already contacted the school," I said.

"What happened?" my dad asked.

Jasmine looked at me and saw how tired I looked. She then began to tell them the story. She left out my theory of it being Scott. When she finished telling the story she said, "Here is my number. Text me when you get home." She passed me a piece of paper with her number scribbled on it.

When she left I asked my parents to drive me home. "What will you do about your car?" my dad asked me.

I sighed, "Well I have to get it repaired. Since they don't know who did it I have to pull the five thousand dollars out of my own pocket. It sucks, but it's life."

"Why don't you just get a new car?" my mom asked.

"This car is better than any of the other cars in the lot. Also the closest car dealership is not a place I'd want to buy a car," I said as I got in my moms car.

"Well it's good I already asked the tow truck to bring it to the shop then," my dad said. He knew I was not stupid enough to get rid of a muscle car. Especially not my favorite model mustang.

"Thanks dad. Do you think I could get an easy job from your work? Maybe I could draw up some blueprints, or even study the history of an area you guys want to buy," My dad was a construction worker who worked both in the office and on the job site.

"I think I could get you a job with blueprints. My firm wants to remodel the park. If I remember right you are going there this weekend, so if you do go you can have a look. I'll have to check with my boss, but I'm sure he'll let you. He liked what you did for him last time," my dad said.

We didn't talk any longer after that, so the ride was silent. When we got to the house I showered and laid down on my bed. I was going to fall asleep, but as I moved my jacket off my bed a paper fell out.

I grabbed it and saw Jasmine's number on it. I quickly grabbed my phone and layed down. I typed in her number and added her to my contacts list. I then sent her a message saying *Hey Jasmine this is Jason.*

It only took her a few seconds to reply *Hey Jason. Remember how you thought it was Scott who ran into you? Well he was the one. Kira caught him grabbing the money while looking at his phone. She took some pictures and managed to catch one of his messages. He was texting Matt. Matt told him that was good driving, and an earlier message said can you drive a car into Jason's. We will be turning these into the cops.*

I Quickly texted back *No we can use this. I'll have Matt pay for the damage and then some and threaten him with it. Don't let on that you, or Kira know about this. I'll tell him I saw Scott walking towards the spot and followed him. Then I'll show him the pictures. If he tries anything again the cops will find out.*

Are you sure? I would really love to tear those two a new one, Jasmine texted.

Yeah. I'm going to sleep though. I'm a little tired from this day, so goodnight, I texted her.

Jasmine replied *Goodnight Jason. See you soon.*

Even though I took that hit I was happy. I got Jasmine's number out of this mess. That was probably one of the best things that happened in my life.

Chapter 8

The Torturous Day

I awoke to sunshine filtering through my blue curtains. The light made the room look like it was glowing blue, but what really caught my attention was the time my alarm clock, that I forgot to set, said. It was twelve thirty pm. I was never one to sleep in. I must have been more tired than I thought I was last night.

I grabbed my phone and walked to the kitchen. I grabbed a bowl, a box of cereal, and some milk. I typed in the password on my phone and saw I had four missing messages. Three of those four messages were from a new number. The other was Jasmine. She wanted to know how I was doing, so I told her good.

I opened up two of the other messages and saw that one was from Antwan and the other from Kyle. They both wanted to know if I was alright, so again I said good.

Before I could open up the last message Jasmine replied *You got a message from the school. It's a video of what happened. It was taken by someone standing in the woods, but it didn't show who hit you, or who took it.*

I quickly opened the video and saw the other car charge right into mine. I winced at the sight of that hit. I'm lucky to be alive. The video also showed that it was no accident though, for it started on the other car.

I texted Jasmine *I might have more proof now. So who shared this.*
We have no idea, but only a teacher or office volunteer could, Jasmine replied.
We texted for a bit before she had to go. When she did, I looked up

the local dealership and saw a picture of the same car in the video. That gave me even more proof, for the car was in a garage that was locked and needed a fingerprint scan to be opened. That meant that Matt's dad had to open it, so the car wasn't stolen. My guess is Matt's dad claimed it stolen later, but in reality gave the car to Scott for this "accident" so it'd look like a robber was the one who stole it."

After that discovery I looked at a list of the office volunteers. One of them was Scott. I also read in the details of the job that any volunteer had access to the schools emergency alert system.

I wrote down all of the details I saw, and even snapped photos for extra proof. The next time I saw Matt we were going to have a talk.

After that I basically did nothing except rest. When I next looked at the clock it said one thirty, so I decided to do something I shouldn't. I got up and grabbed my rental car. I drove it to school and got there at two thirty. Since our school didn't end till four because it started at nine I had time to get to class.

When I walked in the office I signed in while the faculty and volunteer all stared at me like I was a ghost. I quickly asked for a note for my fifth block and ran to the class. When I knocked on the door Ms Lane opened it. I walked in and the whole class was stunned. Jasmine was the first to react. "You're supposed to stay home. Did that accident knock out the little brains that you have left?" she asked sarcastically.

I shook my head and replied, "No one plus one is still eleven." The class laughed as I sat down next to Jasmine. I whispered to her, "I just got bored."

"Wow most kids would love to be off from school, but not you. You must really want to learn," she said back.

"No. I just wanted to talk to some friends and relax. Though my mom will kill me," I replied.

Jasmine said, "There's another reason. You are going to practice to confront Matt."

"How'd you know that?" I was surprised.

"Well it sounds like something you'd do. Plus after that hit you took everyone will look up to you after they see you. And if I remember right, you also have more friends on the team than Matt. You may not think of them as friends, but the way you treated them made them at least like you more than Matt. Matt only talks nice to the starters, and even then it's not really nice," Jasmine explained.

"Well I was just going to do it there because it was the first place I'd see him, but now it's even better. I might need the backup, but if he does try anything I think he'll regret it with or without the support of the others on my side," I replied.

Before we could talk more on the subject, the bell rang. I walked with Jasmine to my mom's class. When we got there, I was glad to see that my mom was smiling instead of frowning. I really had thought she'd tear me a new one if I was there.

I said bye to Jasmine and walked in the class. I sat down and plugged some headphones in. I got started on another drawing for the day and finished it within thirty minutes. I wasn't interrupted by the others who came in the class, but I did see a few surprised faces, especially from the ones at my table.

Once that first drawing was finished I grabbed the one of Jasmine out of my bag and continued to work on it. I added as much detail as I could, and somehow I made the drawing look like it had Jasmine's personality. The smile was bright and friendly. Her eyes were inviting. She had a slight blush in her cheeks.

I was playing my music so loud that I couldn't hear the bell ring. My mom walked over and gasped when she saw my drawing. A movement beside me alerted me that the class was ending, so I slid the drawing back into my bag. I turned and saw my mom who still had not recovered from what she saw.

"That was an amazing drawing Jason. You should enter that in the school's contest," my mom said.

"Well I might, but I think the person that's on it should see it first. I would also have to ask said person for permission," I said as I handed her my other drawing.

I left the class and Jasmine caught me in the hallway. "Hey Jason. Is it cool if I go with you to watch this confrontation?" she asked.

"Yeah," I replied.

As I walked to the field, as I had come dressed in my practice gear for the day, Antwan asked Jasmine, "Why does he look so pissed?"

"You'll find out," Jasmine replied as I caught sight of Matt. I ran to him and said "Listen here you dick. I have proof that you and Scott caused that accident. You can try to deny it all you want, but it's right here," I said, handing him a copy of the proof. "Now I want five grand just for the cost of repairs. If I ever find you near any of my friends again I will personally hand this evidence into the cops. I'll also hand you your own backside and kick your teeth down your throat."

A crowd was starting to grow around me and I saw that over half of them were starters. As a matter of fact all of the starters were there and only Dave, Drake, Antwan, Bryce, Jasmine, and me were the ones not starting that were there.

"Is there a problem," Scott sneered.

Before I could say anything Jasmine said, "You're damn right there is a problem. You are a big problem. If you even take another step forward I'll personally castrate you with a pair of dull scissors."

"Well I could give you the money, but I think I'd rather just beat you," Matt sneered. Most of the starters started to advance on me, but I stayed perfectly still.

"Wow. Am I supposed to be scared?" I asked.

The group that started advancing was met by Bryce, Dave, Antwan, Drake, and two of the starting offense, who later said their names were Nick and Bill. Jasmine tried to get into it, but thankfully Miley was there to pull her back. We were still outnumbered by a few, but we were confident.

Matt and Scott both took a step to me as two more of the starters went after Antwan, who was the most built out of the others. Scott only ever took one step, for he walked right into a left hook that I threw. The hit hit him in the temple and he fell.

Matt got in close and tried to swing on me, but I caught his arm in mid air. As he swung with his other arm I also caught that one. I slammed my head into his head and Matt practically crumpled. As I turned to look at the rest of the fight I saw that Dave had fallen and a second person was fighting Bryce.

I was trying to decide whether to help Bryce or Antwan when a starting defense player said "Now why are there two men fighting Antwan." Everyone turned and saw Xavier standing there.

Matt who managed to get up said, "Good Xavier. Will you help us against the posers?"

Xavier said, "Yeah I'll fight the posers." I cursed Xavier was a man who weighed two hundred and thirty pounds. He was all muscle and stood at six feet and two inches height. There was no way we'd win the fight now that he was helping Matt.

Then surprising everyone Xavier walked over to where the two people fighting Bryce were and punched one of them, instantly laying him out. He did the same to the second guy on Antwan. "The real posers are the ones who can only win by double teaming," Xavier said. After that he stayed back and watched the fight.

Matt said, "Screw him. We don't need him. We still got this." He turned back to me and ran straight at me. That was a big mistake. He swung a wild punch that I easily dogged. I then hit him full force in the gut and he doubled over.

"Now you've messed up, and daddy can't save you now," I said so only he could hear. "You have one more chance to agree to the terms."

"Alright I'll pay it," He said out of fear. I was about to let him go when I heard him laugh. I turned and saw that he was watching Scott grab Jasmine. I swear that with ease I yanked Matt up by his shirt and threw him.

I ran as fast as I could and barreled into Scott. Scott had his arm around Jasmine, but she stayed on her feet while me and Scott crashed to the ground.

Scott looked completely scared as he looked in my eyes. They were burning with anger. I grabbed him by his shirt front and swung a punch after punch into his face. I then said, "Don't you ever touch her or any other girl like that again you scumbag." With every syllable I said a punch connected to his face.

Then coach Wade yelled, "Stop this nonsense now!"

Through my anger I couldn't hear him, so I kept swinging. Antwan, Bryce, and Xavier had to pull me off of Scott.

"What in the hell happened, and Jason if you ever disobey me again you'll be off the team," coach Wade said.

Miley said, "Matt and his posse started a fight with Jason. The guys that were the only ones standing when you got here were helping him.

Then Jason saw Scott grab Jasmine and try to hit her. Jason tackled him and you saw the rest."

She summed it up quite well and everyone who had watched from the stands agreed with her. "Well looks like you're all lucky. No one gets suspended, but if this happens again you'll be punished severely," coach Wade said.

Practice got cancelled and Matt tried to worm his way out of paying my money by leaving early. He really thought he could outrun me. I caught up to him within a few seconds and said "Pass me my money now, or I'll lay you out and rob you."

Matt cursed. "Fine here's the five grand," he mumbled. I counted it before he was allowed to go to make sure it was all there.

After that I walked to my rental and saw Antwan there waiting. "Where's Jasmine?" I asked.

"She is over there," Antwan said.

I ran over to her and asked, "Are you okay?"

She nodded and I could see some tears dripping down her face. I quickly wiped them away and hugged her tightly. "I'm so sorry that you had to be a part of that," I kept telling her over and over again.

When she recollected herself we went back to my car. Antwan was nice enough not to say anything about her crying. I was about to drive when Xavier walked past my window. I rolled it down and yelled out his name.

He turned around and walked back towards my car. "Thanks for the help, but can you tell me why you did it?" I asked him.

"I owed you from a tip you gave me while the third string quarterback was in. Also I hate uneven fights. I also don't really care for Matt, or Scott," He said.

"Well thanks man. You really saved us," I said.

After that I drove to Antwans house and dropped him off. I drove about halfway to Jasmine's house when I pulled over. I grabbed Jasmine and hugged her tight. I promised, "I won't let another guy ever harm you again."

She smiled and said "Thank you for everything."

Before either of us knew what was happening we leaned in and kissed. It wasn't long, but it wasn't a peck either. When we finished Jasmine looked worried. "I'm sorry," she said.

"Don't be," I said. I really wanted to date her right then, but I noticed she was hesitant, so I didn't ask her out. I did however make it sound like that didn't happen by easily changing the conversation.

She smiled at the fact that I tried to make her feel at ease. We fell into a steady, but pointless conversation. I started to drive to her house again. When I got to her driveway I got out and opened her door. I walked her to her door and said bye.

I was halfway to my rental car when Jasmine called out, "Can you come in?"

I turned to face her, and quizzed, "Is that a good idea? I mean I'd love to, but would your parents be okay with it?"

Mrs Kibbler called out, "Her parents are fine with it. As a matter of fact we'd appreciate it if you stayed for dinner."

I smiled and started walking back. "Well ma'am I can't turn down a deal like that," I replied.

When I reached the door Mrs Kibbler pulled me aside and said, "I heard what you did. I'm proud you protected my little girl."

I replied, "It was my fault she was even there, but I'm glad I did protect her. I Didn't think I'd make it in time. I also thought the tackle might have brought her down, but I tried hard not to let it. I still don't know how she managed to stay standing."

"You don't remember your arm holding her up? She told me as your tackle connected your left arm held her up. Maybe in the heat of the moment you didn't realize, but on instinct you kept her up. She would have fallen if not for you being there," Mrs Kibbler replied.

Chapter 9

The Family Meal

After saying that Mrs Kibbler rushed me into the family room. It was a nice room with two comfy looking armchairs, a loveseat, and a couch. They were arranged so that all of them could see the flat screen tv easily. The tv wasn't large, but it was not small either.

I was looking for where I'd sit. I saw Mr Kibbler sitting in an armchair. Mrs Kibbler was sitting in the one next to him, so that ruled those out. Jasmine was on the love seat, and since I didn't want it to be weird I started walking towards the couch.

As Jasmine saw my hesitation she motioned to the seat next to hers. I looked questioningly at Mr Kibbler and he slightly nodded his head. I walked over to the love seat and sat down.

"So what do you want to do after college Jason?" Mr Kibbler asked.

"I was thinking of an architectural career. I do some work for my dad's firm, but I feel like that's not all I want. I love to write, but that job does not have a lot of writing in it," I replied. I've been asked that question many times and never knew exactly what I wanted to do.

"Well it sounds like you're still learning. Do you have any written work? I'm a publisher and I would like to see some of your work," Mrs Kibbler said.

"Yes ma'am. I'm actually working on a new story at the moment," I replied.

"When you finish may I have a look at it?" she asked.

"Yes ma'am. I'll send a copy over when I finish," I said, excited that she was willing to look at my work.

"Mom, you can make him a writer later, but for now leave him relax. He had a long day," Jasmine said, patting my arm.

"No, I had a boring day. I don't know how people can take off of school for fun," I said genuinely.

The oven beeped and Jasmine said, "Let's go eat nerd," as she grabbed my arm leading me to the dining room.

As we entered the kitchen I gasped. The dining room had a stunning look to it. The floor was marble. The walls were a light blue shade. The dining table was crystal clear. The chairs were high backed wooden chairs. They even had a chandelier that shone on the table. The best part in my opinion was still Jasmine, but that would be normal.

"Cat got your tongue? I asked you what you wanted to drink," Jasmine said after nudging me.

"W..water would be nice," I said, still in amazement.

As Jasmine got me water, her mom pulled out some pierogies. She said "These are pierogies. They are shell cov…."

I interrupted her and said, "They're shell covered potatoes. They are also probably the best meal in the world. I love them."

Mrs Kibbler smiled. "It's good to see someone who knows their food well," she said.

"Well I did come from a line of cooks," I replied. That was true. My gram was a chef and so was her mom. My mom could've been one, but she decided she'd rather teach. Her cooking was amazing either way.

I pulled out a seat for both Mrs Kibbler and Jasmine before finally sitting down. I didn't know if they prayed before their meals or not, so I did what I normally would. I prayed over my meal.

When I finished I heard a laugh, and looked up to catch Jasmine covering up a smile. "What's so funny?" I asked.

"Nothing. I'm just not used to people praying over their meal at my house," Jasmine replied.

"Oh. My mom always made me, so now it's a habit," I said, also giving a small laugh.

We didn't talk much as we ate. It probably was because of how good the food was. I didn't eat a lot, but that was only because I was not hungry. When I finished I even said, "I wish I could have these for lunch tomorrow."

"You just made a very good friend," Jasmine whispered in my ear as her mom smiled.

"If you want, I could give you some for lunch," Mrs Kibbler said.

"That would be great as long as it's no burden to you," I replied.

After I grabbed some pierogies for tomorrow, Jasmine walked me to the door. She walked out the door and said, "Look I do like you, but I'm not ready for a relationship yet."

I sensed some deeper meaning in it, but I didn't pressure her into telling me. I knew how bad it felt to be pressured into telling someone what happened. "Yeah. I am not ready either," I replied.

I walked to my car and yelled bye over my shoulder as I drove home.

Songs by The Script started to play through my speakers. I didn't even know I had that many brokenhearted songs on my phone. *Breakeven was followed by Six Degrees of Separation,* and many other songs like it.

Chapter 10

Can This be Suppressed?

I awoke the next morning and quickly got ready for school. I was surprised when I was done getting ready that I was the only one awake. I walked to the kitchen and saw that the clock said I was up an hour earlier than usual.

Instead of going back to sleep, I decided to do something nice. I grabbed two frying pans and greased them up with butter. As I did that I grabbed some eggs and bacon. I quickly set that to cook then set the table. When the food was almost done I started some coffee and made chocolate milk for Olivia.

My parents walked out and asked "What smells so good?"

"I made bacon and eggs. There is coffee on right now, but it will take another minute or two. I'm going to wake Olivia," I said as I jogged up the stairs and helped her get ready. We finished right as the stove went off, so I rushed Olivia to the kitchen.

"Jwason," Olivia complained as I lifted her up.

"Olivia," I mimicked. "If you behave you get chocolate milk and bacon. If you don't you'll starve."

I put her down in her seat and quickly dished out some food. As I finally started to pile food on my plate I said, "I hope you like it."

There was a chorus of how good the food was. My dad said, "What's the reason you did this?"

I laughed out "You're always to the point old man. I did it as a thank you and because I was awake so early."

"Old," My dad muttered. "I'll show you old."

Olivia probably saved my bacon by saying "Dad's like a gazillion years old." Everyone laughed, even my dad.

"Oh by the way Jason I got that job for you," my dad said through a mouthful of bacon.

"Thanks dad. I no longer need the money as much, but I'll take the job anyway," I replied as I got the pierogies ready for my lunch.

"Why don't you need the money as much?" my mom asked.

"Well a guy that was in school caught a video of the accident. He managed to even get a video of who caused it. That person was only willing to pay up before the cops could get involved," I said while hiding some of the truth.

"That's good news, but why didn't you involve the cops?" my dad asked.

"Oh the cops would ruin his record, and he told me exactly what happened. His car was having engine troubles, so he tried hitting the gas hard to get it to work. The car was also not stolen, but being test driven," I replied while I grabbed the keys of the rental off of the hooks on the wall.

I had to leave early, so I could get my car out of the shop. I know it's surprising that they could fix a car that fast, but they had all the parts.

When I pulled up to the garage I saw my car sitting out in the open. There wasn't even a scratch on it. This place had done a miracle in my opinion. I was glad to go back to my beautiful car. I traded the guy the keys of the rental for my mustang.

Soon as I got the keys I jumped into the car. I drove to my house and picked up a happy looking Olivia. "Yay. Jwason got his car back." she said as she got placed in her car seat.

"Of course I got my car back. I'd have even given you to the guy who fixed it if he needed some more money," I replied as I tickled her.

I ran to the driver seat as fast as I could. I wasn't worried about being late. I just couldn't wait to feel the car underneath me as if it were alive. I turned the key and the engine roared to life.

"Livvie what type of music should we listen to?" I asked as I hooked my phone up.

"Can we listen to Ne-yo?" she replied.

I turned it up and took off to her school. When we got to her school we repeated the same process as monday. When she was out of the car I basically cruised to my school.

I got to my school with about ten minutes to spare, so I stayed in my car. I was surprised when I heard someone knock on my window. I cursed when I saw it was Kayla.

I had no choice but to ignore her. I had to go to class, but I knew that this twisted girl would be following me. I got out of the car and slammed the door.

"How are you doing Jason," Kayla said as a statement.

I turned to her and snarled, "I'm doing good. No thanks to your friend. I managed to come to school yesterday. Now can you please leave me alone. I have no feelings for you and never will. Can't you tell that. I'm not just another guy you can get. I'm the guy who would rather die than be caught hanging out with you. So bye."

Thankfully she just stood there as I walked by her to class. I put headphones in and waited for class to start. I was also hoping that the music would get rid of my anger.

Jasmine walked by Kayla and laughed. She hadn't heard a word, but she did see that I was the one who made her look stunned. She walked in and frowned at seeing me listening to music.

She walked over and sat next to me. As she was sitting down she saw that my song that was playing was more of a hate song than a normally happy song. That made her frown.

She pulled out my earplugs and I almost snarled at her before I realized it was her. She said, "These are not allowed. You can't possibly think I'll let you miss any of my jokes at your expense."

I smiled and said, "Oh. Are you sure you just don't like Mrs. Lola's favorite student picking on you."

Jasmine said, "Why would I pick on myself?"

Mrs Lola was a life saver. "How's my favorite student doing? I heard that you were in an accident," Mrs Lola said.

Jasmine just looked shocked. As Mrs Lola walked by I mouthed *thanks*. "Hey Jaz you might want to pick your mouth up off the floor and close it before bugs fly in it," I said.

It wasn't the best career move as Jasmine smacked me really hard.

I'm not going to lie, but if I had the choice between Matt hitting me or Jasmine hitting me, I'd choose Matt.

"Jeez with an arm like that I'm surprised nobody is throwing roses at you," I said.

"First of all I didn't hit you that hard. Secondly it would be asters not roses," Jasmine said.

"I'll make a note to remember that. Don't worry though, because unlike you my notes are taken quickly," I said.

Really another bad decision. I got slapped again. As a matter of fact, I was left with a red mark that time.

The next two days of school went by fast. Not surprisingly I had a couple more bruises than I thought I should, but Jasmine sure liked giving them.

Before we left, I said "I'll pick you up at eight so we can go to the park."

After that was said I quickly drove home. I went through my closet looking for something nice to wear. I know it sounds weird, but I wanted to look nice for Jasmine. I was falling for that girl more than I had thought was possible.

I was ready long before the date, that wasn't a date sadly, began. So I decided to finish my drawing of Jasmine. It was nowhere near done when I started, but I did finish it before I had to leave to meet Jasmine.

I was going to leave it, but my mom's question about entering it in the contest changed my mind. I was going to show it to her anyway, so why wait.

With thirty extra minutes to spare on the clock I drove to the nearest florist shop. I bought some asters and a vase. I made sure that I got a half and half mixture of pink and purple ones.

Finally I drove to her house and rang her doorbell. I put both hands behind my back to hide both the flowers and drawings. Jasmine opened the door and my eyes nearly busted. She was wearing a pair of shorts and a tank top. I was not used to seeing her without jeans on, and her beauty made me feel stupid.

Jasmine said "Are you going to stare all day Jason, or are we going out?"

I said, "I'd love to do both, but first I got something for you." I pulled the asters from behind my back and handed them to her.

Jasmine smiled, "Thank you. I'm surprised you remembered."

"Of course I remembered. I had to take a mental note to remember," I said glad that it made her happy.

"Of course you did. Thank you so much. You're the first person to ever do this for me," she said with tears in her eyes.

"Well..... I ugh..... got you something else to, but this isn't to keep for now," I managed to say. I grabbed the picture and showed it to her.

"Wow. That's an amazing picture," Jasmine said.

"My mom wants me to enter it into the competition, but I told her I needed your permission," I replied.

"Why do you need my permission?" She asked, oblivious to the fact it was her.

At that moment Mrs Kibbler walked to the door. She took a look at the picture and asked, "Did you draw this Jason?"

I nodded. She beamed and said, "You made an amazing picture of my daughter."

Jasmine was shocked. "Wait this is me?" she asked.

"Yes Jasmine. That's why I needed your permission," I laughed.

"Of course you have it Jason," she replied. She handed her mom her flowers and said "Mom can you please put these in my room while I go out?"

Her mom smiled and did as she was asked. I walked Jasmine to her door and opened it. "I still can't believe you open my door," Jasmine said.

"I still can't believe I'm the first to buy you asters," I replied.

"Thanks for that," she said as she quickly kissed me. Not a friendly peck on the cheek, but a romantic one on the lips.

"I think the thanks are all mine after that," I said as I walked over to the driver seat.

We talked about nothing that was important on the way. That still didn't stop the ride from being a good one. I was just happy to be sitting there talking to Jasmine.

I knew I was falling for this girl, but I also knew that she wanted me to wait for her to be ready. I actually thought I'd never be ready to date again until I met her. I thought I'd stay brokenhearted, but things change.

Jasmine and I were the first from our school to get there, so we just waited. The park was beautiful, but I saw why it needed to be redone.

The benches and some of the playsets were falling apart. Without even realizing it I started to plan for how I'd want the park to look.

I'd change some of it, but for the most part it would just be replacing. The only thing I'd actually add would be a basketball court and a few more benches. At eight fifteen the place was only lit by moonlight. I liked the effect, but I would add a few lights around the play areas.

I was actually so into my thoughts on how'd I redo the park that Ms Lane surprised me. "Ahh, it's nice to see two partners come to these events,"

"I'm glad to be here," I said smiling. I'm sure that Jasmine being there was the main reason I liked being there, but there were more reasons.

Jasmine smiled and said, "Me too."

Ms Lane just smiled as she walked off. Once she was gone though I grabbed Jasmine's hand and started to walk around with her. "I'm glad you're the one showing me around Jaz," I said.

Jasmine replied, "Well it was either me or Kayla, and seeing how much you like her I wasn't going to let that happen."

"Ew. I'd never like her. Looks aren't the most important thing, but it's nice when they match the personality. Kind of like yours," I said blushing.

"You look cute when you blush," she said.

I laughed and said, "I'm still nowhere near as cute as you."

We walked around the park at least once before the stargazing began. Me and Jaz walked over to a telescope and took turns looking into it.

One of the times I swung it to face Jaz, and said, "Wow this is the best sight so far." She slapped my arm, but couldn't hide her smile.

As everyone started leaving the park me and Jasmine sat down on a bench. "This was my favorite night so far," Jasmine said echoing my thoughts.

"I completely agree," I said as I grabbed her hand.

"You're making it really hard for me to stay single," she said.

"I could say the same," I laughed out.

We kissed right after that. It was probably the best kiss ever. In it I felt her passion and love for me. When she pulled back I could tell she made a mistake.

"Jason I'm sorry, but that wasn't supposed to happen," she said.

"It's okay. Would you like to go back home?" I asked her, trying to get rid of the tension.

"Yes please," Jasmine replied.

We walked to the car and I opened her door. I then drove her home, but stopped at her mailbox, so she could get the mail.

I could instantly tell something was wrong as her face fell into a frown. I saw on the top of the paper that it said the name of Matt's dad's company. "When are you supposed to get your next car payment?" I asked.

"Not for another week," she said.

"God dammit," I yelled. "Matt's trying to make sure you leave me alone. I knew this was something this prick would do."

Jasmine just said, "It's okay. I'll pay it."

I dropped her off at her house, but quickly looked at the return address on the paper. I drove to the dealership in anger. I saw that the lights were on and ran to the door.

Now most people won't believe this part, but it happened. I slammed open the door and walked over to the guy at the counter. "Where is Matt," I growled.

"My son is back there, but if you think…" Matt's dad said threateningly raising his hand in a fist. He would have kept talking, but when I pushed him backwards he shut up.

I charged through the door where Matt was and saw Matt, Scott and someone else.

Matt laughed out, "This fool wants to get beat up."

"This fool is going to kill you," I growled. The trio walked towards me with metal tools in their hands. Scott attacked first, but his attack only connected with the floor as my fist hit him in the temple, dropping him.

The other guy walked slowly towards me. That caused me to back up against a wall. He swung thinking I had nowhere to go. He was wrong. I ducked to the right and grabbed his wrist. Before he could yank free I elbowed him in the gut and then smashed my palm into his chin.

Matt probably did the smart thing. He threw the tool at me and grabbed another. I caught the first one, and waited for him to throw the second. When he did I caught it. He was waiting for my throw, so I threw both the tools and missed on purpose. Matt tried to grab them and never heard my approach. I grabbed him by his throat and choked him.

"Next time you make someone I know pay early on their car I'll kill you," I growled as I slammed his head into the wall.

I walked out of the building and laughed as I saw the cops were there. "Hands above your head," the officer said.

I did as he said, but before he could put handcuffs on me I said "Watch the footage. I did everything in self defense."

The cops walked in the building and managed to get to the surveillance room before Matt's dad could delete the footage. They watched and let me walk free after asking who had to pay up early. I told them that it was Jasmine, but she wasn't the only person who had to do it.

Instead of going straight home, I went to the park. I sat on the bench with a piece of paper in my hands and started drawing out the way I'd redo the park. It calmed me down enough that I could drive home. I stood up and was surprised to see Jasmine sitting at a bench not far from mine.

I tried to walk by without letting her know I was there, but I guess she knew I was there. "Jason come here," she said in that sweet voice.

I walked over and Jasmine gasped. "What did I become uglier?" I asked.

"No, but you're bleeding badly," she replied.

I put a hand to my face, and felt blood on my face. "Crap," I said.

Jasmine stood up and passed me her jacket, which I declined. I grabbed my own jacket and held it to my head. We sat in silence for a bit. Jasmine broke it by saying, "The cops told me what happened. They said I wouldn't have to make another payment on the car again, and that I was lucky to have you as a friend."

"I wouldn't say lucky," I replied.

We sat in more silence, but this time I broke it. "Well I know you said you weren't ready, but I now am. I was heartbroken from my ex. She cheated on me with my best friend. Or I thought he was my best friend. The dude had the guts to brag about it in my face. He was lucky that the guy that was my actual friend pulled me back."

I took a break to catch my breath, and thankfully Jasmine didn't ask a question. I continued, "I had thought that she would be the one for me, but of course she wasn't. She just wanted to be in the popular section in school, so she used me like a stepping stone. I'm glad for the one friend that stayed by my side. If it was not for him I'd have probably been expelled from school. He saved my future that day, and I'll forever be in his debt."

Jasmine sensed that I was done talking without a nudge, so she asked, "What about the girl?"

"Abbie, for that was her name, never saw me again. She tried to apologize through texts and calls, but I ignored it. It was the best thing I could do. Me and Jake, who was the guy that became my only friend, were the outcasts. Nobody talked to me or Jake. We stayed to ourselves, but Jake had always been like that. We stay in touch, but I feel bad that I left him there," I muttered.

"Hey It's not your fault. He understands, and he probably even told you it'd be the best thing you could do," Jasmine said while squeezing my hand.

"Well that's my story. I'm glad I got it off my chest. You don't have to tell me your story because I told you mine. I just wanted to get it off my chest," I said.

Jasmine hesitated for a second, but she started her story, "I dated a guy back when we were freshmen. He was a sweetheart, or so I thought. He was one of the jocks, but his leg gave out on him that year. We dated for most of the year, but Kayla got jealous. She couldn't have someone be more into me than her."

"I kind of expected that it would happen. Kayla started flashing more skin at Josh, my ex, and flirting with him. I tried as hard as I could to stop it, but I knew it would happen. He started to get intimate with Kayla when I wasn't around. When they finally went all the way, Kayla recorded it and sent it to everyone. She just used him to make me mad like always, so I don't go out anymore with people. She tries to turn them against me. She thought she'd be able to keep all guys away from me, but only a few actually did. They all tried to sleep with me, which was normal, but I turned down everyone who asked me out. I didn't want Kayla to turn them on me," Jasmine said through tears.

I brushed her tears away and held her close. "That guy was an idiot. He could've had the best person in the world, but instead he chose a whore. Do not let Kayla feel accomplished by this. If I had the choice, I'd have chosen you every time. Kayla is an attention seeker, and a rude person. You're the best," I said, hugging her tightly to me.

The words I spoke were the truth and Jasmine could tell by glancing at my eyes. She smiled and kissed me on the lips. "Thank you Jason," she said.

My whole heart poured out into hugging the girl of my dreams. I may not have known it at first, but I was in love with her. She was the most important person to me. I'd probably have robbed a bank for her. Instead I just decided to kiss her again.

"I'll always have your back," I said as I got up and grabbed her hand. "Is your car here, or did you walk?" I asked.

"I walked," Jaz replied as I helpped her up and walked her towards my car. I opened her door as always, but this time I kissed her as she sat down, before closing the door. I walked to my side of the car and hopped in. I grabbed my phone and prayed it would finally stop playing heartbreak songs. It didn't disappoint. *Perfect* by Ed Sheeran started playing.

I could've cheered. Me and Jasmine were dating. My phone was off of sad songs. I even had for the first time in a long while felt like I was cared about.

Chapter 11

That Was a No

I could probably have floated all the way home. I was so happy by the simple fact that me and Jasmine were dating. I drove her home slowly. Not because I was afraid of crashing, but because it gave me more time with Jasmine.

Jasmine didn't seem to mind. She kept glancing over at the same time as me, and we would smile as our eyes met. I was just glad she was as happy as I was about this.

As I pulled into her driveway, her parents came outside. Mrs Kibbler said, "Hey Jason."

"Hey Mrs Kibbler and Mr Kibbler," I said as I opened Jasmine's door.

"Thank you for what you did. We really appreciate it," Mr Kibbler said.

I grabbed Jasmine's hand and walked up to her parents. "It was no problem. Both Matt and his dad had it coming. Anyone would have done the same," I said.

Mr Kibbler looked surprised, but Mrs Kibbler smiled. "Are you two a couple now?" she asked.

"Yes Ma'am," I replied.

"It's about time," Mrs K said with a smile. "I knew from the second I met you this would happen Jason."

"Tell me why I have a feeling that my mom will say the same about your daughter?" I asked.

"Jason, you must have the wrong person. Your mom is probably praying you don't get stuck with this adult sized child," Mr K replied.

I laughed hard. It wasn't the smartest idea, for Jasmine hit both me and Mr K. I can't tell you how hard she hit Mr K, but she did leave a bruise on my arm.

"Yeesh. You'd think I learn not to mess with the lady. It's like stealing candy from a baby. It's fun, but if the parents catch you, you get pounded on," I said rubbing my arm.

Jasmine started to hit me again, but I caught her arm. "Now you messed up big guy," Jasmine said as she tried to hit me with her other arm. I also caught that one and picked her up before she could kick me.

"Now what are you going to do?" I asked a squirming Jasmine.

"This isn't fair," Jasmine complained. "You could throw me across the yard. I couldn't even lift you."

"That didn't stop you from trying to fight Matt," I replied back.

"Let me down," Jasmine ordered.

"Not unless you say please," I said in a voice that sounded like I was chiding a child.

Jasmine had other ideas though. She flashed me puppy dog eyes. I will admit to giving in, but if you saw her puppy dog eyes, you'd be surprised that I relented to let her down for a full minute.

"Well he at least tried to teach Jasmine some manners," Mr K said.

Before Jasmine could smack him I grabbed her by her arm. "No more hitting your dad. You cause enough pain for him without physical violence needed," I said.

I got another slap, but Mr K gave me a thumbs up, so it was worth it. Mrs K thankfully interfered before I could get to many more bruises. "Jasmine leaves Jason alone long enough that he can say goodbye before leaving," she said.

"Does he have to go?" Jaz asked.

"Yup. My mom would be worried if I didn't get home soon, and I really don't want another meeting with the cops today," I replied. I didn't really have to go, but Mrs K clearly wanted me to go home now, so I gave an excuse.

"Aww. That sucks. I was hoping to talk to you for a bit longer," Jasmine pouted.

"I'll call you when I get home, but for now, goodbye," I said kissing her on the forehead.

"Bye Jason. I'll be waiting for that call," Jasmine said.

Once I got in my car I quickly drove home. I may not have drove seventy miles per hour at fifty miles per hour zone, but I did get home in record time. The second I got home I walked upstairs and started to dial Jasmine's number. I got about halfway through dialing her when my mom called me.

"Hold on mom. I'll be there in a second," I replied as I finished dialing Jasmine's number.

As the phone was ringing my mom asked me, "How did the stargazing go?"

"I liked it, and I think Olivia would love it. If you want one night I could take her out for a weekend to stargaze. You know to get us out of your hair, and to give you and dad alone time," I replied just as Jasmine picked up.

"Hello?" Jasmine said.

"Hey Jasmine. I made it home perfectly fine," I said.

My mom smiled when she heard Jasmine's name and said "I'd love you to take Olivia out, but let's talk about that later. Say hi to my favorite student."

"Jasmine my mom says hi. She also called you her favorite student. I think she was lying, but I don't know," I said into the phone as I grabbed a water.

"Is she still there?" Jasmine asked.

"Yeah I'll hand her the phone," I replied.

I passed my mom the phone ignoring the danger warning going off in my mind. My mom and Jasmine talked for about a minute before I got smacked twice by my mom.

"Ow! What was that for?" I asked while rubbing my arm.

"One was for making fun of Jasmine, and the other was for saying that I lied," My mom said, passing me back the phone.

"Thanks mom," I replied sarcastically. I just managed to dodge the next smack.

I walked to my room and once there I said "Jasmine you, my mom, and me can never be in the same room together. I get smacked enough as it is by you. I don't need two sets of bruises."

"Awww. Poor baby. Do you want me to kiss them to make them feel better?" Jasmine asked.

"No," I replied instantly. "You would just hit them harder."

Jasmine laughed out, "Your right. I would totally hit them harder. By the way, I can't wait to see you play the scrimmage game tomorrow."

"Oh I umm… forgot about it. I need to tell my family. When they come maybe we can tell them we're together," I said.

"Once you win the game we will tell them," Jasmine said confidently.

"Hopefully I get put on the second stringers team then. I have a feeling that the first stringers are gonna let any ball I throw be intercepted, or even let the defense right on through," I said nervously.

"That does sound like the first stringers. I also don't think you will be able to stay first stringer. You have the skill, but Matt's dad will make the coach pay up," Jasmine said.

"That may be why I didn't tell the cops that they were doing it to the coach. I wanted to be on the second stringer team. Plus from what I can tell the second stringer team is a lot better than the first stringer team offense wise," I said.

"Well I have to go. My phone is about to die. Goodnight Jason," Jasmine says.

"Goodnight Jasmine," I replied. Once she hung up the phone, I put my phone on the charger, and walked to the kitchen.

My mom and dad were in there, so I asked, "Would you guys like to come to the scrimmage game tomorrow?"

"Of course we would," my mom said.

"What time does it start?" my dad asked.

"The game starts at two, but the band starts at one. All entries are free," I said.

Once we had everything set, I headed to my room to sleep. I laid in my bed trying to sleep, but I just couldn't fall asleep. Finally I gave up and walked outside to the back of the house.

On the first day of school I had set up my punching bag outside. That's where I walked to now. I started pounding on the bag to get rid of all of my excess energy. After about an hour I went back to my room. I laid on the bed and my last thought before I fell asleep was that I was finally dating Jasmine.

Chapter 12

The Scrimmage Begins

I awoke at seven in the morning. It was not a surprise, for I was always an early riser, but I just felt like going back to sleep. I laid down and just closed my eyes when I heard my vibrating phone go off beside me.

"What in the world is wrong with you?" I ask my phone. Thankfully it didn't reply, so I picked it up and saw that I was getting a call.

Surprisingly when I answered the phone I was pleasant. "Hello," I said, stifling a yawn.

"Hey this is coach Wade. Jason I hate to tell you this, but you will be playing second stringer during the scrimmage game today," coach Wades gruff voice said.

"That's amazing coach," I said.

Coach Wade said, "What do you mean it's amazing?"

I laughed out "Two reasons. The first being that the first stringers would make me look bad, so Matt could play first stringer. The second is that, from what I could see on the field during practices, the second stringers are better."

"Kid you have a good eye, but we never had this conversation. I'm sure a few second stringers will become first stringers today," coach Wade said before he hung up.

I was tempted to go back to sleep, but I thought better of it. I did my normal morning routine, and after that I grabbed a pen and a piece of paper to write a note telling my mom that I was going out.

After the note was thrown on the table I grabbed a gym bag, and threw some water in it. Once the bag was full I ran outside towards the park. It was a nice long run that got my blood flowing, but wouldn't leave me tired afterwards.

I was tempted to go to Jasmine's house, but I decided that I'd just leave her a goodmorning text. I was walking back when I saw a vehicle pull over. I walked over and asked "Do you need some help?"

I was surprised when MIley answered back. She said, "No, but me, Kira, and Bryce thought you'd like a ride back."

I know I went on the run to get my blood flowing, but let's be honest here, who wouldn't ride in a car with their friends over walking home all alone.

"Thanks guys," I said as I got in the back.

"It's no problem. I'm guessing since you ran here that you don't live far from here," Miley said.

"Speaking of not living far from here, Jasmine lives real close to the park. When we were kids we'd always go to her house after playing at the park," Kira said.

I smiled at Jasmine's name, and Bryce caught the quick flash of teeth. "Oh. What's so funny Jason," he asked, raising an eyebrow questioningly.

"I have no idea what you're talking about," I said, but my voice betrayed me as it went extremely high pitched.

"Ohh. I think I'd like to know what you're hiding Jason," Miley said, and sadly the other two chipped in.

I flipped Bryce the bird and said, "Well, as it turns out my girlfriend lives really close to the park. It's actually the house closest to the park that she lives in."

Kira said, "Jasmine's house is the closest to the park." It took her a moment, but she finally connected it. "Wait you and Jasmine are dating. I can't believe it!"

"I can't believe it either. I have to keep pinching myself to make sure I'm not dreaming," I said.

"Well did she tell you why she wouldn't date you earlier?" Miley asked.

"Yeah, and if Kayla ever tries messing with me like she did to Josh, I have a feeling she'd regret it. First of all I'd turn her down. Secondly,

I have a feeling that Jasmine would kill her for trying to mess with me. And thirdly, She might have good looks, but she is nowhere near as beautiful as Jasmine. Jasmine's beauty is not just on the outside, unlike Kayla's. Jasmine is beautiful on the inside," I said.

Bryce instantly killed the girl's tears from how romantic I had just been by saying, "The guy is whipped already."

I could've and probably would've killed him had Miley not fired back, "At least he got some then. And if you keep it up you won't get some for a long time."

"Well I didn't get any, but that's not the most important part of a relationship," I said as Miley pulled onto my road. I got out and said bye before running back home.

Upon arrival at my house my phone chirped as Jasmine replied to my goodmorning text. I opened the door as I thumb typed, *Hey sleeping Beauty*, to Jasmine.

I walked about three steps before Jasmine replied, *If you keep calling me names, even good ones, I'll make you too hurt to even walk.*

Sorry, beautiful. How are you doing?, I typed as I walked into the kitchen.

Jaz typed back. I'm *doing very well. A handsome man started dating me last night.*

Oh. I got replaced that fast. That wasn't even fair, I replied.

Now I see that I might have hit you too hard last night. I was talking about you, you handsome man, Jasmine replied.

I laughed out loud and replied *I think you need some glasses. I'm really ugly.*

No you're not, Jasmine replied.

I'm pretty sure you and my mom would disagree on that one, but I'll leave you alone for now. See you later bye, I texted as I sat down on my couch.

Jaz replied bye, and I just turned on my tv to catch any good movie. Sadly none were on, so I resorted to going outside. I couldn't do what I really wanted to, which was to swim, because it was cold out, and my pool wasn't set.

I did manage to distract myself by throwing a football in the air and catching it. At some point Olivia came out to throw it with me. She may not have been the best practice partner, but at least it was fun to watch her try to play.

An alarm on my phone went off, and I jogged to my car. I grabbed

Olivia and drove off to the football field. My parents were not going to leave until later, but I was bringing Olivia along because she wanted to see Jasmine.

We reached the parking lot just as Jasmine pulled in. Before I could even say hi Olivia jumped out of her seat, and ran to hug Jasmine. Jasmine smiled and said, "I missed my favorite person in the whole world."

I shot Jasmine a hurt look, as Jasmine winked at me. "I thought your favorite person was Jwason," Olivia said.

I laughed out, "At least somebody agrees that I'm your favorite."

Jazmine raised her eyebrow and replied, "I think you're both delusional."

"What's dalushunal," Olivia asked.

With my quick wit I replied, "It's the word a big meanie uses to say someone is crazy in a bad way. It's a swear word."

Sadly Jasmine was quicker and said, "It means you are believing a lie that someone you care about told you. So if you listen to your brother you're delusional."

"Who would you believe Olivia, your brother or a person you met only once before," I asked, playing my ace up my sleeve.

"Well Jwason is my brother, so I choose Jasmine," Olivia answered.

I pouted, "I'll remember that when you want any ice cream, cotton candy, or toys."

Olivia started to pout but Jasmine asked, "Would you like some cotton candy?"

As expected from any seven year old Olivia nodded, but the unexpected part in my eyes was when Jasmine turned to me. "Jwason can you get me and Olivia a cotton candy, " she asked while giving me puppy dog eyes.

I was about to say no when Olivia tugged on my sleeve and showed me the same expression I gave in. Now if you ever heard this story told from their view they'd say I'm lying, but I will only say that if you'd been there you'd know who was lying.

I walked with them to the food stand and got three cotton candies. Before I could take a bite Kira said, "Thanks for the cotton candy," as she ripped my cotton candy away from me.

Before I could snatch it back she took a bite. "Why do I even try to get myself something nice," I complained.

The girls looked at each other and said in a baby voice, "Aww does the baby want some cotton candy?"

I nodded my head and saw Kira pick some of her cotton candy. Her arm flicked back and forth while I moved sideways. I managed to dodge the flying snack and let off a sigh of relief when Olivia decided she'd throw all of her cotton candy at me.

I caught it out of reflex and handed it back to her. "Wow you're lucky I caught that, or you would have been cotton candy less," I said.

Olivia replied, "uh-uh you'd have gotten me another one."

The third offering of cotton candy was by far my favorite. Jasmine passed me hers and I took a bite. "All better now Jwason," Jasmine asked in that darned baby voice.

"Better but not perfect," I copied in her baby voice. Then in my real voice I said, "A kiss always makes it perfect."

"I'll kiss you to make you feel better," Olivia said.

I crouched down next to her and she kissed my cheek. "Now I'm perfect," I said though I'd have rathered Jasmine to kiss me.

"Perfect," Kira asked, raising her left eyebrow.

Jasmine butted in and said, "Not yet." She kisses me first on the cheek, then after a few seconds of my silent pleading she kissed me on the lips. "Now he is perfect," Jasmine announced and I had to agree.

Sadly that nice moment was ruined by Olivia asking, "Can I look yet?"

Kira laughed out, "You can. The nasty people are done with the nasty romantics."

"You girls really know how to ruin a moment don't ya," I asked.

Jasmine answered, "Yes they do."

Before the girls could deny what we said Miley and Bryce showed up. "Hey ladies and Jason," Bryce said.

When we all said hi I introduced Bryce, Miley, and a belated Kira to Olivia. Of course Olivia liked them instantly as all seven year olds did.

"Oh by the way Olivia when you meet Kyle and Taylor you might need to cover your eyes. They can't stop with the nasty romantics," I said.

"Uh at this point I will have to walk around with my eyes closed," came her cute reply.

Before she could turn around and look at me I pecked Jasmine on the lips. After a quick sign from Bryce I grabbed Olivia and turned her away, so Bryce could kiss Miley.

"You know we could make a good team Jason," Bryce said.

I laughed out loud, "Only if I could teach you to catch."

"Well I caught all types of ugly passes in the gym," Bryce retorted.

"I still have the best catch," I said holding up Jasmine's hand.

Bryce replied "Nah you got the worst one." That little comment earned him four slaps and a punch. All the girls slapped him, and I was the one to punch him.

"Why are you all hitting on Bryce when I'm over here ladies," Antwan yelled as he jogged over with Christie "Well all of you but Jason could hit on me."

That earned him the hardest hit of that night from Christie. "Calm it down Christie. I'll need that tight end to catch the game winning pass tonight. Anyway he's just trying to make you jealous. If he was serious he'd have asked me to hit on him," I said winking.

"Sometimes my boyfriend is a little full of himself. I'm sure you girls know what that's like," Christie said. I laughed when both Jasmine and Miley nodded.

"You know we could say…" Bryce began.

"If you like being able to move without hurting I would suggest you don't finish that sentence," I interrupted.

"Jason the wise," Kira said.

"I quite like the name, though I doubt I'm wise," I replied.

Jasmine quickly said, "At least you're smart enough to know that."

"Well lets be honest here. If I hadn't been that smart you wouldn't be with me now would you," I asked in an innocent voice.

Kyle's deep voice said, "If she we're smart she wouldn't be with you."

"The only part I can argue about there is that she is smart. Way too smart for me maybe," I said.

"Definitely too smart for you, but I'm hoping it'll rub off on you," Jasmine's barbed reply came.

Kira came to my defense by saying, "At least he has some bright moments."

Jasmine's reply was great. "I guess I did rub off on him already."

"Anyway to end this conversation Kyle, Taylor, Antwan, and Christie this is Olivia. Olivia these are most of my friends," I said.

"Hi Jwason's fwends, " Olivia said.

"Anyway I believe some quarterback tried to change the subject about how he got smart. If I remember right, we got to the conclusion that Jasmine gave it to him," Kyle said.

"Kyle if you don't leave Jason alone I'll castrate you," Taylor said.

I mouthed a thank you and said, "Please tell me that you guys are done picking on me now."

Antwan replied, "We'll never be done picking on you."

Olivia turned to him and raised her fist up like she'd hit Antwan. Jasmine laughed "Looks like a little seven year old would disagree. And if you're even half as smart as Jason you'd know to run or stop."

Antwan laughed, "What's she going to do? hit me?"

And as every little kid does she threw a temper tantrum. Antwan tried covering his ears, but me and Bryce grabbed an arm each and stopped him.

Thankfully Antwan gave in and apologized to both me and Olivia. Taylor was smart and asked, "Do you think I could borrow this little monster when Antwan annoys me?"

"That's up to her. But I doubt she'll let you because she knows Jasmine always needs backup now that we are dating. She will probably have a busy day hissy fitting," I said. Olivia nodded her head to my statement.

The rest of that hour passed by in a blur as my friends met my parents. After that me and Antwan went to change into our gear, and got ready for the game.

When we got to the field Dave, Drake, and Xavier were waiting for us. I asked, "You guys ready for a win today?"

I was surprised when none of them answered yes. It wasn't until the game started that I found out why. I saw Matt talk to the freshmen kids on our side of the game.

I just waited for the game to begin nervously. I had pregame jitters and knew that I would lose them as soon as the game began.

The coinflip happened and we got the ball first I watched as the kick receiver team ran to their positions and waited.

The ball was kicked and flew right into our kick receiver's hand. Jack, the kick receiver sped down the field. He got tackled on our forty for a thirty yard gain. Now I ran to the field.

Chapter 13

The Scrimmage game

I was now in game mode. Plays ran through my head as I got in a huddle. "Guys," I said, "Let's test Antwan's skill in catching. Drake follows him closely cutting diagonally left. Dave goes exactly opposite them. Everyone knows the plan?"

Everybody nodded though the linemen looked hesitant. All of the linemen were new to the team, so they were the ones Matt talked to.

Of course Matt had made a deal with them. It was that if they let the first stringers through that he would give them a first stringers position. Of course it was also a lie.

When we hiked the ball I was instantly tackled. "What's going on," I asked as we huddled. I noticed the linemen were looking at their feet and Antwan just shook his head.

"It looks like you boys let them through, and I believe it was a lie that Matt told you. If you guys want to be on the team as first stringers you gotta play to win. This conversation should not be repeated, but the coach already told me that most of the first stringers should be replaced. If you want those positions, play the game you love to win," I said.

"He's right," Antwan said, "we must earn our places on this team and I don't know about you guys but I'm gonna be on the first stringers team this year."

We went for the same play and this time I was not instantly rackled. The play ran through just as I thought it would. Drake's and Dave's line gives Antwan plenty of space in between him and his guard so I passed him the ball. No sooner had the ball left my hand when someone tackled me.

The tackle didn't hurt too bad thankfully. Antwan caught the ball apparently, for the crowd was cheering, and I stood up just in time to see him cross the touchdown line.

I got off the field and watched as our kicker missed the field goal. I mean there was no hate from our team, but we sure and hell as could've used it. As our defence took up position I noticed that they all were determined unlike our offense. Matt and his team put up a good fight but they could not get a touchdown.

Once back on the field, my team made another touchdown. The field goal was good and that put us at 13 points to 0.

Matt hit the field and ran a 50 yard touchdown. Their kicker made the field goal so we were stuck just one touchdown ahead.

The kick return went horrible. The kick receiver caught the ball and made it to the thirty before he hot tackled. The problem is when he got hit he dropped the ball. Matt's team got the ball, so we practically gave them that touchdown.

The kick receiver apologized for what happened but we told him it's okay. The next play was just as disastrous. I was making a running play when Matt switched to defence. I still kept the play and ran the ball only to get tackled by Matt and one of his teammates.

The ball fell loose, and when everyone else went for the ball Matt kicked my right ankle as hard as he could. "If you were smart you would stay down," Matt said.

I tried to stand up, but my ankle couldn't hold the pain so I fell back down. The only one who saw what had happened was Jasmine. She yelled for the coach to come get me. Once I was carried to the bench, by the coach, the medical examiner checked my ankle over.

"Your ankle will be fine, kid," one of the examiners said. "You are just not allowed to play for a bit."

"Great, our best QB just went down," Coach Wade said under his breath.

"I'll be in before you know it," I said, hoping it would be true.

Matt's side got the ball and made two touchdowns, but they couldn't make a field goal.

Matt's team was two field goals ahead of ours at this time. My defense managed to stop them on their ten, so we had an advantage. The backup QB was starting to run in when I called him over.

I said "You're doing great out there man."

The backup, who I later found out was named Bryan, said "Thank you, but we all know I'm not as good as you."

I laughed at that. "You are as good as me, but your mind isn't racing with new plays like mine. If you'd like a play to run here, try to send all of your men on the left side, and follow behind Antwan," I said.

Bryan nodded his thanks and ran out to complete my play. The play worked like a charm. Bryan scored the touchdown.

By sheer bad luck the kick receiver on Matt's team lost the ball and Xavier grabbed the ball. Bryan quickly made another touchdown play to tie the score.

Matt's team got the ball to the thirty and made a field goal. They only did it so that they had a chance at winning, but they had two reasons that they didn't. The first being that they left two minutes on the clock. The second being the fact that I was ready to play.

I hopped out on the field after our kick returner got us to our thirty. "Boys, did you miss me," I asked.

The answers I got were some that are not polite to say, but they were all in the negative. "Well hopefully you can catch my ugly passes, cause I refuse to lose this game," I shouted.

I called a very unexpected play. I guess that's why it worked. I called for a backyard football play. I passed to Antwan, who backwards latteralled it to Drake after gaining 20 yards. Drake ran it for ten more yards before having to lateral it to Dave. Dave made it ten before he was about to get creamed by someone, so I called for the ball.

I thought I would get creamed as well, but I managed to make it to the touchdown line okay. If I am to be honest, the only reason I know that I did cross the line is by the loud roar the crowd made.

It didn't last long though because a second or two after I crossed the touchdown line, I got solidly tackled to the ground hard.

I stood up and was all fine afterwards, but, before anyone told me what happened, I could not tell you who tackled me. The person in question was Matt of course, but when I was taken to be examined, I couldn't tell them what had just happened.

There was a large fuss about me and my having a possible question, but for some reason I couldn't tell what was being said.

That all changed when Jasmine ran down the bleachers and practically leaped over the fence. She came to me and asked me if I was okay. I nodded my head, which was a big mistake, for I got really nauseous. It also made me plan on never doing it again, and with that thought I nodded my head. I instantly regretted that and realized I had already broken my plan.

Out of the corner of my eyes, I saw players leaving the field. "Why is everyone leaving the field," I asked Jasmine.

Jasmine looked a little startled as she replied, "You don't remember crossing the touchdown line to score the final point?"

"I scored the final point? Are you joking with me," I asked.

The look that crossed her face told me that she was not joking. *What in the heck happened,* I thought. My brain could feel where the memory was, but it could not replay the memory in my head.

As that thought passed through my head, the medical examiner was shining that dang flashlight in my eyes. Like always I wince at the light, but unlike normal, I couldn't keep my eyes open.

"He will need to go to a hospital. He has a concussion and from the look of his ankle his ankle is broken," the examiner said.

"I don't feel any pain in my ankle sir," I said. From the look on everyone's faces I could tell that I should. I looked down and understood why. My ankle looked like it was twisted at about a 45 degree angle.

I think I may have blanched out a little because Jasmine's grip tightened on my hand. "Jason, are you okay," Jasmine asked.

"I don't know," I replied, being as honest as I could.

"Just relax kid, you will be okay," one of the coaches said. So following orders I laid against Jasmine, and said, "This good enough sir?" That made her smile slightly. I even think the coaches smiled too. I probably would have, but any slight movements hurt my head.

"Yes it does," coach Wade said. While this was all happening the examiner had gotten me ready to go into the ambulance. The coaches looked at each other before I was put in the ambulance. Finally coach Lane said "Kid when you come back we will need a starter. You up for the job?"

"That depends on whether or not it involves more of these visits," I joked right before the door closed. I was glad to see the person accompanying me was Jasmine. She was holding my hand on the drive and it was really nice.

Now you may think I'm crazy thinking it's nice and all when only pain should be coursing through me, but adrenaline really helps. To be honest I could only feel a dull pain. I know that soon that would change, but then I was happily bliss.

Happily bliss is a great thing to be. I sat there with the love of my life, even if I didn't know it then, holding her hand while her fingers were running through my hair. I don't care who you are, the feeling of your loved ones fingers running through your hair is relaxing.

Relaxation kills adrenaline, or at least I believe that's what killed my adrenaline. The pain came rushing through my body in a second.

Chapter 14

Broken

I guess the pain caused me to blackout, for I didn't remember getting to the hospital. I awoke in a hospital bed with a hand on my shoulder. There was another hand on mine, but I had a guess that it was Jasmines.

As if to back my thoughts up, Jasmine leaned into my view, dragging our hands along, and said, "He's awake doc."

"No I'm not," I mumbled.

The doctor chuckled. "If you're not up will pour ice on you," he said.

"You do that and you may not live," I said half joking. Thankfully he didn't put ice on me. I was about to rise when I remembered my foot was broken. I started to lift the sheet that was covering me, but the doctor stopped me.

He said, "You should be okay to walk, but you will need support. Your foot looks fine, but relax it as much as you can."

"That I will do doc," I said. I got up to a sitting position and grabbed the crutches beside me.

My mom, who had been waiting in the room, told me to go to my car and dad would drive us home. So I hopped over to the car with Jasmine in tow.

For the first time I wasn't the one to open the door for Jasmine. She opened my door, in the back, and helped me get in. Once I was in she hopped in beside me. Olivia was sitting in the front. She turned her head and asked/yelled, "Are you okay?"

"Yes he is. He just needs to be in a quiet car," Jasmine said. Bless her for knowing how to get Olivia to shut up.

I layed against Jasmine's arm while my foot rested in the seat. I'm glad she didn't complain because if she had I would have been sad. She was really comfortable, and god did her fingers running through my hair felt great. I could have stayed there forever, but I got home before forever.

Thankfully Jasmine was able to call home, and get permission to spend the night as long as we were in different rooms. And of course we were, because my parents are also strict in that matter. She helped me to my bed, and then sat in a chair beside it.

"What am I that bad you can't sit next to me," I asked her.

"No it's not that you are that bad, but I don't want to hit your ankle," She said.

"You won't hurt me," I said.

She laughed, "I may not but, I don't want to see you bawl like a baby."

"Hey I only cry like a baby every other day," I playfully whined.

"Aww would the baby like some cheese with that wine," Jasmine said, causing me to laugh.

"Actually I'd prefer some more wine with it if you don't mind," I said, rolling to the left to dodge the hit that Jasmine clumsily swung at me. "Well on the bright side I can dodge your hits while crippled," I said.

What a big mistake. Jasmine quickly slapped me twice as I tried to squirm around. "What was that about dodging," Jasmine asked as I was trying to get back to a comfortable position.

I replied, "I said that you could easily take advantage of hitting a crppled"

God I really wanted to be in more pain today, I thought, right before Jasmine's hand hit my shoulder. As if to echo my thoughts, Jasmine said, "You really want to be hurt more, don't you?"

"Apparently so," I said. *Get your crap together,* I thought to myself. I was hoping that that would help me reset my filter, but I'd have to wait to see if it did.

"How are you doing over there cripple," Jasmine asked.

I replied, "Trying not to hop off to sleep." The score is 1-3 in favor of no filtering. At least the filtered side was getting a point.

Jasmine smiled and said, "Does the baby need some sweep." God that baby voice drove me crazy. Thankfully God was on my side and installed a great filter for me.

"Yes the baby needs some sweep. But the baby needs a piwow to sweep," I said in my baby voice. Thankfully I didn't get hit, but I did get a pillow. Jasmine passed me a pillow from the chair next to my bed.

"Well time for baby's nap," Jasmine said in a feigned sadness.

I nodded my head and said "Goo goo gaa gaa."

God must have given up on me because a pillow was flung at my head. Before I managed to say something else, however, a couple clogs moved and I stayed quiet.

"Goodnight," I called out as she shut my light off.

"Goodnight cripple," Jasmine replied.

I awoke in the morning with a pain in my ankle. Thankfully somebody had put my pain meds on my nightstand. There was also a cool glass of water beside my meds. I grabbed my two pills, and swallowed them with the water chasing them down. Instead of getting up instantly, I laid in bed for about thirty minutes.

I probably would have laid there longer, but the smell of hot cocoa and bacon drifted through the crack in my door. Being an athletic person, who is always hungry, I arose to first brush my teeth, then go grab some breakfast. I was at the entrance to the kitchen when I heard Jasmine's laugh.

"Wow everyone is partying while the crippled sleeps. I see how it is," I joked as I walked in the kitchen.

"Well when someone makes breakfast for you, you tend to forget about tiny problems," my dad said.

Looking around hopefully, I replied "I'm not a tiny problem. I'm a big one and I need food. Is there any chance there's any left?"

"Nah your dad ate it all," my mom said

The crushed feeling I felt was instantly dispelled when I saw Jasmine reach behind her and pull out a plate of bacon and scrambled eggs. "The cocoa is in the kettle Jason," my dad said.

Of course I was a big kid, so I filled a mug with cocoa and put a handful of the miniature marshmallows into the drink. Don't judge me. Cocoa is not just for kids. That's just Trix.

As I was eating my lovely breakfast, I was watching Jasmine getting along with my family. She made Olivia laugh throughout the whole time by making faces, She kept talking with both of my parents and managed to even keep my dad interested. That was not an easy thing to do.

Wow she fits in really well, I thought to myself as I finished my meal. I started to wash my dishes when my mom said, "You don't have to do that today. You're not supposed to be on your feet."

"Of course I shouldn't be, but someone has to do the dishes," I said.

"Someone should, but your mom would like clean dishes," my dad said.

"Is that why she never lets you do them then?" I asked.

That was not a good idea. Dad kicked me, playfully of course, and walked out of my reach. I of course tried to follow him, but my injury prevented me from catching up to him. My dad got that cocky smile that said he had won, but a smile touched the corner of my mouth.

"Olivia, will you do something for your favorite brother," I asked.

"Yup," Olivia said.

"Well there is a big, mean, old troll standing over there that I can't get to. Would you mind hitting him," I asked while pointing at dad.

She charged at dad as an answer. Dad put a mock face of horror on as she charged him down. Olivia ran into dad, but before she hit him, dad picked her up.

That's okay with me because she was just the distraction. With Dad completely distracted, I snuck up on him and hit him and limped away. I would've gotten away with it if it hadn't been for the meddling Jasmine. She smacked my arm. I shouted, "Ow."

Before I could react any more she dragged me to Dad. The worst part was when she said, in an innocent voice, "Here is the trouble maker that hit ya."

The Betrayal was real. I was so hurt emotionally that I didn't even feel the smack my dad gave me. Instead of chatting with my family, I walked over to the door and walked outside. I sat on my porch and waited for the noise of footsteps following behind me.

When they came, I said, "Unless you're here to apologize, keep walking."

"Aww is the baby upset," Jasmine mocked.

I was about to reply, but she stopped me by sitting beside me on the porch swing and giving me a kiss. "Baby accepts your apology," I said through a smile.

I definitely accepted the second kiss. We could have been sitting there for an hour but it felt like seconds. We were just holding hands and chatting about random things on the porch.

Olivia came out shortly after me and Jasmine stopped talking. "Jwason come play tag with me," she shouts out.

I Start to rise as Jasmine laughs. "It's cute that you think I'm the only one that's going to play with her," I say as I grab my crutches.

"I'll play gladly. I'm just laughing at the thought of you trying to catch me while on crutches. You could barely do it without them," Jasmine replies.

"Wow, you really know how to kick a guy when he's down," I laugh.

Jasmine quipped "Your not down yet, but I'd love to see you try to get back to your feet."

Olivia said "You'd pick Jwaon up though."

"Nah the wicked witch would leave me waiting for help," I said as Jasmine got up.

"If you aren't careful the wicked witch will hurt you," Jasmine said while glaring at me.

I joked, "You and what army."

Olivia ran to Jasmine's side and said, "I'll help her."

I faked scared, or at least that's what I tell myself. "How would it be fair for the double trouble to attack me," I asked. Olivia tagged my leg and took off for the hills as an answer. I just hobbled after her and was slowly catching up to her when Jasmine picked her up and ran off.

Of course, being an athlete, and not wanting to be a spoil sport, I ran after Jasmine. I dropped my crutches at some point, but I didn't care. Well I didn't care then.

I reached Jasmine within a few minutes, which was surprising considering I was on a bad foot. Then again, Jasmine was also carrying the additional 50 pounds known as Olivia.

I tackled Jasmine softly, making sure she'd land on me. I then started tickling both of the girls. That's where the caring for the crutch began. Olivia rolled onto my foot and the pain shot through me like a bullet.

I'm proud of the fact that I kept my shouted words clean. "Son of honey, bisquits that hurt. Mother fluganuga," I shouted out. Olivia rolled off of my foot as soon as I started yelling, but the damage was done. I clutched my ankle while I writhed around in pain.

Jasmine took control. "Olivia go get your parent's and bring the crutches back," She said in an authoritative voice. Olivia obeyed as Jasmine tried to get me to relax. "Come on Jason. Just stop grabbing your ankle and let me help," Jasmine continues.

Her voice slowly broke through the barriers of pain. Once they were broken, I stopped clutching my ankle and looked at her. She had a forced smile on her face, which I saw right through. She tried to hide her fear that I could have this pain forever. "I'm good," I managed to say.

Jasmine forced a laugh. "You are anything but good," she said.

I shook my head and said, "You're here. I'm definitely more than good."

Before Jasmine could reply, my dad and mom rushed up to us. "This may hurt," my dad said as he started to help me up.

"Son of a…..," I started to say, but I stopped myself in time. My dad got me up to my feet so he was on my left side. I put my left arm on his shoulder and slowly walked, using my dad as my crutch. We walked towards where Olivia was looking for my crutches.

As we got there, Olivia found my last crutch. She came bounding up to me and dad with the crutches in her hand. She gave them to me, but a little hesitantly.

"I'm sorry Olivia. I wasn't mad at you. I was just in a lot of pain," I said.

She nodded her head and gave me a quick hug before dashing off. *Kids,* I thought to myself. With my crutches supporting my weight, and my dad slightly behind me, I hobbled to the porch swing. Well hobbled is being a kind word. I kind of flailed to the porch I guess.

Once on the swing, I laid my injured leg on a conveniently placed cooler. My parents tried to go into full protective mode, but I waved them off. "Guys i'm fine. I just need to rest my leg," I said.

Eventually, the worried four, became a quiet Jasmine. She was just sitting there beside me, in total silence. Her silent company was quite nice, but eventually I had to talk to her. When did we start talking? I have no idea but the quiet changed to a conversation.

The conversation was important, but not the words. The conversation showed me that Jasmine was there for me. She was willing to wait for me to talk about what's on my mind.

That evoked a feeling deep within me that I was at first surprised to feel. I was feeling loved, and I was helplessly falling in love. The way that Jasmine was making me feel with just a few simple words and just her presence, was amazing.

There are stories of love at first sight. I do believe them, but it'd be a lie to say it was love at first sight. You may have loved them from the first moment you laid your eyes on them, but you didn't know you loved them until a certain moment. That moment for me was probably when Scott first tried to hit Jasmine.

And of course I've been having moments of where I knew I loved this girl, but the feeling of being loved by her? That was the best feeling in the world. That feeling made me feel invincible. That feeling made me feel stronger than I actually was.

Now all of those thoughts were flying around in my head while we chatted. Jasmine was a major distraction to my filtering of thoughts, but, thankfully, God was on my side here as he made sure that I didn't say I love you.

I mean I'd love to tell her that I love her, but I didn't want to rush things too much. That would be a real easy way to ruin the relationship as I see it. Since that relationship is definitely the most important thing to me, I'm not trying to ruin it.

Eventually my brain tuned back in with what Jasmine was saying. "So there is an end of summer party coming up and I was wondering if you'd like to go with me. It also marks the end of the first semester," Jasmine said.

"I'd love to go with you, but I must warn you, my dancing skills are horrible, and I may accidentally step on your toes. Now if you can accept those terms, I'd love to go with you, and if not, well, I'll blame the reason you said no on me being crippled," I replied.

Jasmine jested, "Crippling depression does not count as being crippled."

"They don't need to know the depression part, only the crippled part," I replied.

"And what of Olivia? Will you lie to her as well? I'm sure she would be very upset with you," Jasmine said.

"No fair. You cant use my own sister against me," I pouted.

Jasmine replied, "Say's who?"

I said "Say's your date to the dance."

"I thought you were gonna step on my toes? I can't take you if you'll step on my toes," she said.

I shook my head and said, "No worries, I would never do anything to hurt you intentionally."

"I'll hold you to that one buster," she replied.

I asked, "So when, and where is this dance?"

"Well It's supposed to be next Saturday and at the school, but we are trying to get it to be inside the botanical gardens on sunday," Jasmine said.

"Anyway I could help with that," I asked her.

"Well not really. We need to get the school to agree to it," she explained.

"What if we got a petition with a bunch of students signatures on it? Maybe even see if we can get the botanical gardens to let the school do it there for free, or a discounted price," I said.

Jasmine smiled. And that smile was the most beautiful smile I've ever seen. "That's an amazing idea Jason. We could swing by the gardens later today, and make the petitions tonight," Jasmine said excitedly.

"You could use my car to go to the gardens whenever. It's not like I'll be able to," I said.

"What, you don't want to walk around the beautifully romantic gardens with your girlfriend? And here I thought you were romantic," Jasmine said.

"I am romantic. I just don't think it will be a good idea to hobble around beautiful flowers when I could fall at any moment. Also I don't want people to see you with an idiot in public. It'd make people think you are even crazier than what you are," I said.

Jasmine stood up and crossed her arms over her chest. With a stern look she said "You are not getting out of going with me mister. I don't care how many excuses you give. I'll carry you if I have to."

I just smiled and said, "Do you think you could carry me around the gardens?"

"No, but I know after I start struggling you will start walking," She said matter of factly.

"Dang. You know me too well," I complained, as I stood up. I walked into the house and yelled, "Mom, I'm going to the botanical gardens with Jasmine. We will be back in an hour and a half."

With that said we got into my car, and for the first time, I didn't open Jasmine's door for her. Once we were in my car, I hooked up my phone and hit shuffle on my playlist. Music quietly played as Jasmine turned the key to start the car. With the engine roaring, the car started the drive to the botanical gardens.

We didn't talk on the ride there, but occasionally we'd sing the chorus to a song that would play, but other than that we were quiet.

When we arrived at the gardens, I was speechless, which coincidentally was the song playing on the radio.

When I could finally lift my jaw off the ground, I said, "Wow this place is amazing. It would make the perfect place for the dance. Especially if we have it so around the middle of the dance the sunsets. We could have it go from three to eleven, so we can watch the sunset behind these beautiful flowers."

Jasmine raised her eyebrows to make them look like a question mark. "Are you done yet," she said.

"Not at all, but I think I should save my ideas to help persuade the person in charge. And that's the only reason. Totally not so you don't hit me," I said as I grabbed her hand and started, kind of walking. We took our time walking to the office, stopping every now and then to stare at the flowers. Now I know it's cheesy, but the most beautiful thing in those gardens was Jasmine.

Standing there, with a smile on her face, and the sunlight shining through her hair, she was beautiful. The light also made her blue eyes shine, and the mischievous twinkle in them was slightly more visible.

I now understand the song *Eyes On you* by Chase Rice. That Moment with my eyes on her was perfect.

When we reached the office area of the gardens we saw an elderly man walking out of the building. "Excuse me sir, do you know where we can find the manager or owner of these gardens," I asked him as he started walking past us.

"It so happens that you are talking to the owner young sir. What can I do for you and the lovely young lady here," he replied.

"Well sir I am Jason, and this lovely lady is Jasmine. We came here today to see if there was anyway you could help us kids at Ridgeback Highschool with our end of summer party. We would love to be able to hold this party here in your gardens but the problem is we couldn't do it without your help sir. We'd like to know if you would be willing to give us students a free or discounted rate to rent this place out for a night. We would have supervisors at this party so kids shouldn't get too out of hand," I answered.

Jasmine continued, "We would make sure no alcohol or drugs got onto your property and we would make sure that there was a cleanup crew to clean any trash we may miss."

"Sir we would just like a chance to help our class experience the beautiful sight of the sun setting over the flowers. This would help us out, but it could also help you out. If our school had this dance here you would gain more publicity," I said.

"And more publicity means more money.more money leads to a longer time of running this place," Jasmine said.

The owner looked at us and let a smile break out on his face. "With all of this persuasion I couldn't possibly say no. Though in truth I would have let you guys have it here anyway. I went to Ridgeback myself and it is an amazingly beautiful place, but definitely not a place for a dance," he said.

"Thank you so much sir," we said in unison.

"The name is Bob. You two make an incredible team. You guys should do this more often. You would be able to convince anyone," Bob said.

"If only that were the truth. We still can't convince my little sister to do her homework," I replied.

With Bob's guidance we toured the gardens and talked about plans for the party. Thankfully, since Bob has rented the gardens out a few times before for parties, we didn't need to bring our own tables and chairs, for there were plenty of them there.

As we were just about to leave, Bob asked us "Have you guys already got a DJ?"

"No sir. We were gonna look for one tomorrow," Jasmine said.

"I know one who would do the job for free. He's an old friend of mine. I could ask him for you, if you want," Bob said.

"That would be amazing. Thank you so much for this sir," I said.

"It's my pleasure sonny. I love helping out my old school. That place gave me so many memories," Bob said with a far away look in his eyes.

We said our goodbyes to Bob and headed back to my house. On the trip home we started talking about the dance. We started getting different committees planned, like the clean up crew, the set up crew and the decorators. We even started to plan on how we could bring this to the teacher in control of events.

Chapter 15

The Dance Setup

Jasmine couldn't spend the night again, which sucked in my opinion. She did at least get to stay for dinner, After we finished eating some amazing beef stew, Jasmine told our parents about the dance plans we had so far.

They both liked the idea so far, and my mom even offered to help us if we needed it. And that caused another idea to spring to mind. "Well there is one part we did forget about. We need supervision or else it wouldn't be able to happen. Would you like to be one of the supervisors," I asked her.

She smiled and said, "I would love to honey."

The conversation slowly shifted away from the dance after that. Me and Jasmine excused ourselves and went to sit on the porch.

We just sat there and talked excitedly about plans for the dance and even got committee sign up sheets ready.

Then, all too soon, the light started to fade as the sun set. "Well I have to get home," Jasmine said.

"See you tomorrow I guess," I said as I kissed her on the forehead.

I watched as her car's headlights, which my parents got earlier today, disappeared before I headed inside.

Once inside my house I laid down on my couch to watch Tv. At some point I must have dozed off because I woke up to the sound of an alarm going off. I looked at my phone and saw that it was five am so I quickly got my clothes together and took a shower.

Taking a sower with a bad ankle is not fun. It hurts quite a bit, but at least I was getting clean.

After my shower I started making a bowl of cereal when I got a text message from Jasmine. *I will be there at seven thirty to pick you up crippled.*

Oh how nice of you to carry the crippled, I replied.

Jasmine just replied, *You wish.*

True to her word, Jasmine pulled into my driveway at seven thirty. I walked outside carrying just my bookbag and saw Jasmine getting out of the car. She gave me a hug and walked into my house. "What are you doing," I asked her.

"Well you are supposed to use your crutches, so I'm grabbing them," she said as she walked back out carrying them.

"I was hoping you forgot about those. They're really uncomfortable," I complained.

"Well looks like you'll have to be uncomfortable," Jasmine said as she got in the car.

Once we were at school we walked to class and talked to Mrs. Lola. We told her about the dance pans and she was more than happy to help supervise. She even let us put up some sign up sheets for the committees in her class.

The day passed by very fast, until lunch time. While we were on the way to lunch, we saw some of Matt's friends laughing at me. That didn't really bother me, but that was before I knew why they were laughing.

When I sat down with the lunch bunch is when I found out what they were laughing about. Antwan came out towards us and said "Have you guys seen the video."

"What video," I asked.

He answered by showing us the video. We all watched the game winning point from the game saturday. It showed me scoring the winning touchdown, but then it showed me getting picked up and slammed to the ground by Matt.

"So that's what really happened," I said.

Jasmine was furious. "Why didn't the ref call that. He was sitting there watching it. And who recorded this. It'd have to be someone on the field. How did you get this video Antwan," She said rapidly.

"Matt sent it to the whole team. I wouldn't be surprised if Jason didn't get it," he replied.

Of course I checked my phone and saw the video there. "Well at least we know what really happened now. I wouldn't be surprised if everyone in the school saw this before the end of the day," I said.

Jasmine wanted to keep talking about the play, but she stopped when I mentioned the dance. The whole lunch bunch agreed to help setup and help takedown the dance.

On the way to pre calc class I could tell Jasmine was still upset about the video. So I stopped her in the hallway and said "Hey don't worry about that video. Like I said it's already getting around the school, but the only ones laughing are Matt and his gang. Everyone else is giving me looks of amazement and sympathy."

"That doesn't mean that I don't want to neuter him," she said.

I hugged her and said "Feel free to do that anytime. Just please don't do it to me."

She laughed. God I love that laugh. In a happier mood we walked towards class and I carried the crutches just to hold her hand as we walked.

Apparently the news was even spreading to the teachers. Mrs. Lane made that apparent when she looked surprised to see me. "Are you sure you should be here Jason," She asked, her voice filled with concern. "I saw that hit you took, you shouldn't even be walking right now."

"I'm perfectly fine ma'am. The doctor said I could come to school. How did you see the hit though," I asked.

"Someone sent it to all of the school. Everyone here knows about it. And seeing you walk it off like the way you did made you look like a hero," she said.

"I wasn't trying to look like a hero. I just wanted to go home," I said before I took my seat.

In my last class I could tell my mom saw the video. She looked pissed. I thought she may have neutered Matt if she saw him.

Thankfully the day ended, or so I thought as I heard my name called over the announcements to the office.

I walked to the office and was surprised to see the coach and Matt sitting in there already. I walked in and heard the principal tell Matt he was suspended for a week.

Matt walked out angrily and the coach asked me "Boy did you send that video to everyone?"

"No sir. I found out about it during lunch and apparently by then so did everyone else," I said.

"So you didn't try to make yourself look like a hero," principal Owen asked.

"Hero? How would I look like a hero. All I did was take a hit and stand up after it," I said.

The coach answered for me. "That hit should have been a more serious injury. The fact that you stood up after it was amazing. There aren't many people who could do that," he said.

"Well, since I'm here coach, and you're the one in charge of events, me and Jasmine found a better place to have the dance. We were going to hold it in the gardens. We've already started putting committees together to help the event run nicely. Any chance we can do it sir," I asked him.

"Once those committees are full let me see them, but as of now I'd say it sounds good," he said.

"Thank you so much. I'll send you the lists as soon as I can," I said. "Well if that's all I guess I'll be heading out then."

The principal nodded his head, so I walked out the office, and walked right into Jasmine. "Sorry, I didn't see you there," I said.

Jasmine replied "Maybe if you would use your eyes, you'd be able to see me."

"Maybe if you were just an inch or two taller, I said.

Wham.

"Okay," I said, rubbing my arm where she hit it, "I totally deserved that. What are you doing here?"

"Well, the group told me you were called to the office, so I decided to wait for you out here," she said. "You could at least say thank you."

"Thank you m'lady," I said, taking a bow. I then ruined the effect by saying "Was that good enough?"

"No it's not, but we can't wait for you to perfect it. There is too much work to do. Me and the other female members of the lunch bunch came up with two possible themes for the dance. The first is the sunset theme, where we try to match the decor to the colours of the sunset.

The second is the garden theme, where all of our decor has something to do with the gardens and all of it's bright colours. We are sending a petition out tomorrow to see which one we should do. We also thought it'd be a cool idea to have a summer court that the students could vote for. Have a summer princess and prince from each grade, and a summer queen and king," Jasmine said.

"That sounds amazing," I began.

"But," Jasmine said.

"But, don't we need to get this announced immediately if the dance is this saturday? Otherwise people wouldn't have time to vote," I finished.

Jasmine said "Yes we do, but how are we gonna do that?"

I smiled, "Well the principal and coach Wade both liked the idea. I'm sure they wouldn't mind us announcing it. So we need to write out what we will say and have the votes done by Friday morning in class and count them before saturday."

Jasmine raised her eyebrows inquiringly. "Are there anymore plans floating in that head of yours," she asked.

I nodded and said "We need to plan what we are wearing and I need to go shopping for dress clothes, but, other than that, no."

"Oh my god," Jasmine shrieked. "I totally forgot to get something to wear for the dance."

"Well you could take me to get my clothes and go dress shopping," I said.

Jasmine shook her head. "I'll take you clothes shopping after I go dress shopping. I don't want you to see me in my dress."

"Wait are we getting married," I asked.

"No I just want you to be even more excited at the dance," she said.

As we were talking, we walked out to the parking lot. "I'll always be excited just to be with you," I said as I opened her door for her.

"Well you will still have to wait to see my dress. It will be a pleasant surprise," Jasmine said.

We continued talking as Jasmine drove me home. She dropped me off, but she didn't stay over. She instead decided to go dress shopping with her mom.

The rest of the night flew by in the wink of an eye. I did a few leg workouts that are supposed to help my injured ankle recover. They seemed to help some, but I didn't really expect them to do much at quickening my recovery. The rest of the night was spent with my family, whether it was playing with Olivia, or chatting with Mom and Dad.

The next morning, I was awoken by my phone vibrating on my bedside table. I reached my hand out groggily and grabbed it. I looked at it and saw it was a call from a random number. I was about to ignore the call, but seeing as it awoke me I answered it.

"Hello?" I yawned out.

"Hey, is this Jason," a female voice said. She sounded familiar, but I couldn't tell who she was.

I replied "Yeah, who is this?"

"It's Kayla," came her reply.

I was instantly awake. "What in the hell do you want? And How did you get my number," I asked her.

"Well you wouldn't let me tell you about your friends, so I decided to tell you over the phone. And Jasmine gave me your number," she said.

I laughed. "Do you really think I'd believe Jasmine would do that. She despises you. And My friends are way better than you could ever be. So please leave your lies after the beep. Beeeep," I said as I hung up.

Of course she called me back but I just let it go to voicemail. Matter of fact she gave me three voicemails, all of which i didn't listen to as I got ready for school.

As a matter of fact, I wasn't planning on ever listening to those voicemails, and they slipped my mind until lunch. Kira asked me "Did you ever hear the voicemail I sent you? I was trying to talk to you about the dance."

"No. Sorry, I just thought your call was one of the many that Kayla gave me," I said.

Jasmine turned to me and I could see the anger on her face. "Why didn't you tell me Kayla called you?"

"I'm sorry Jasmine. It slipped my mind. This morning she woke me up by calling me trying to tell me bad things about my friends, but I just ignored her and hung up. She left me three voicemails after that I guess. I originally thought it was four. If it makes you feel any better I haven't listened to any of them yet," I said apologetically.

Jasmine still looked mad, so I said "Why don't you listen to the voicemails? Knowing Kayla, she'd probably get mad at being ignored, and will still try to tell me bad things about you guys."

"Of course you want to hear what Kayla has to say," Jasmine spat out.

I grabbed for her hand, trying to hold it, but she just smacked my hand away. "Jasmine you know that's not what I meant," I said.

She wouldn't listen though. She was fuming and was ignoring me completely. To make matters worse Kayla called me at that moment.

Jasmine looked at my phone and saw the number on it. "Why don't you answer it. We all can see you love her," Jasmine said.

Before I could say anything Kira said "Stop being a prat Jasmine. He clearly only has eyes for you. Everyone here can see how he feels for you so why don't you ease up on him."

Jasmine glanced around and saw that everyone was nodding their head in agreement. That wasn't making her mood better though, and I guessed why. The whole group knows what Kayla did to Jasmine, everyone does. Only the original lunch bunch knew how bad it hurt her.

"Hey guys, do you mind leaving me and her alone for a minute," I said.

The others moved a bit away as Jasmine just sat there looking mad. My phone stopped ringing by then. "Jasmine I know you're really insecure that I would leave you for Kayla, but I won't. Not only do I not like her and people like her, but she did something that makes me despise her. And I'm not talking about the lies or anything she did to me. I'm talking about what she did to you. She hurt you bad. And she keeps trying to hurt you. And her mistake was hurting someone that I love. And I'm talking about you Jasmine. I'm crazy, helplessly, in love with you. Nothing Kayla could do can change that," I said as I looked in her eyes.

I could tell I was getting to her so I wrapped her in a hug. Then, my phone decided to ring again, the little betrayer. Of course it was Kayla again. Jasmine saw it too, and I could see all of the progress I had just made faded. So I answered the phone with "Kayla stop calling me. I will never want you. I'll never hug you, or kiss you, or do anything with you. I hate you and I always will. You hurt the one love of my life, and I'm not gonna let you do it again. So stop trying. You're just making a fool of yourself." With that said I hung up the phone.

Jasmine's eyes grew wide with surprise. She never thought she'd hear anyone talk to Kayla that way, or even choose her over Kayla. A tear started to fall down her cheek. "Are you okay? Did I say too much," I asked her, filled with concern.

Jasmine just shook her head as I pulled her into a hug and wiped the tear away. I held her tight to me for a few minutes before she said "I'm crazy in love with you too."

I smiled and said "I don't think I've ever been this happy."

"Just wait for the dance, mister," Jasmine teased.

"Just wait for me to step on your toes, you mean," I joked.

"If you step on my toes I'm gonna stomp on your bad ankle," Jasmine replied.

The rest of our crowd came back, and thankfully Jasmine and Kira were perfectly fine. "So what did you want to talk about for the dance, Kira," I asked.

Kira glanced away quickly and said "I was gonna ask about where we would get the food from. Like who's gonna cater us?"

I could tell that's not what she really wanted to talk about, but, nevertheless, it was an important topic. I thought for a few seconds and then asked, "Does Jacked Fries cater?"

"Well they do, but only their standard foods. And burgers and fries aren't the best meal for a formal dance," Taylor said.

I was disappointed for a moment, but good news came out of it. Kyle said "Well my mom runs the place, and she has them cater our family events with other meals. Maybe she would do this for us."

Jasmine said "We could even keep the burgers and fries for those who are more relaxed and want a good burger."

"I'd get one," I said, while staring pointedly at Jasmine, "but I have a feeling someone would get mad if I got grease on my dress clothes."

I wouldn't get," Jasmine started to say, but Kira interrupted her.

"You would kill him in a heartbeat if he ruined you special dance night," Kira said

For the rest of the day I wondered what Kira had wanted to talk about. Finally in art class I asked her about it.

"Well me and Miley were both trying to ask you if you were going to do anything special for Jasmine," she said.

"I have an idea, but it's gonna take some work. I was planning on playing, and singing the song *In case you didn't know.* I was also going to get her a bouquet of roses with half a dozen asters," I said.

The girls looked at each other and Miley said "Why that song?"

"Because I'm crazy about her," I sang out quietly.

"The guy's have all been planning something secretive. Do you know what it is," Kira asked me.

I nodded, but didn't say anything. In fact, us guys found out that the DJ was Bryce's uncle and we all picked a song that we wanted him to play for us. There was another surprise, but you'll learn it later.

For the rest of art class, the girls kept trying to get me to tell the secret. I didn't, surprisingly. The bell came to my rescue, and as soon as it rang I was on my feet and heading for the parking lot.

Jasmine met me there. "Are you ready to go shopping, crippled?"

"That depends on if you'll carry me through the store," I replied, getting into her car.

"I'll put you in one of those carts you push kids around in," She said.

"Pinky promise," I asked her in my, probably poor, kid imitation.

She smiled and put her pinky up in the air. "I pinky promise," she said.

"You do know you'll have to do that now, right? As a member of the pinky promise council, I am to enforce all pinky promises," I said.

"Just shut up before I push you out of my car," she said.

"You wouldn't dare," I said.

"Oh, wouldn't I," She asked with an eyebrow raised.

"No you wouldn't. You wouldn't risk breaking your car door," I said.

She laughed. "I wouldn't want to break my dance partner either, even if he's a kid at heart."

"You know, judging by your tone, that sounded like an insult, but it feels like praise," I replied.

Jasmine feigned a hurt look and said, "Me? Hurt you? No, I would never dream of that."

As said, many times before in this story, I am a little slow on the uptake, but even I could pick up on that much sarcasm. "You know, sarcasm suits you well. It almost makes it seem as if you're not a nice person," I said.

She gave me a sideways glance. "Who told you I was a nice person? I don't remember being nice to anyone," she said.

"Well Olivia did, but you could have bribed her," I teased.

"I would never bribe Olivia," Jasmine said. During the conversation, we had been driving to a mall. We just pulled into the parking lot as she said that.

Jasmine led me around the mall like she had been there millions of times, which she probably had. She brought me to the mens dress clothes area and picked out a shirt in the shade of blue she wanted me to wear. I grabbed a shirt in my size and tried it on in the dressing room along with a pair of dress pants.

I came out to show off the outfit to her, and she gave a low wolf whistle. I blushed and the lady running the dressing rooms laughed.

Chapter 16

The Dance

The days before the dance passed in a buzz of excitement. People voted for the summer court, and the ones who signed up for jobs for the dance put hours of work into getting it set up.

Sunday morning arrived and I got ready for the dance. I went out and bought asters for Jasmine, and even managed to find a corsage to match my blue shirt.

The day was going by agonizingly slowly as my family kept asking me if I was ready. Of course I said I was, but, in reality, I was the farthest thing from it. I was nervous that I'd mess up somehow and ruin things with Jasmine.

Finally, after what felt like years, it became the time for me to leave to pick up Jasmine.

My leg had healed to the point where the doctor said it was okay for me to drive, however, it still hurt when I walked too fast.

I drove my mustang to Jasmine's house and walked to the door and rang the bell. Her dad answered the door and said, "Now comes all of the threats and promises I'm supposed to make to make it seem like I hate you, when I actually care for you."

"Seems right to me sir," I replied, or I tried to say. The words at the end may have become a weird sound because at that moment Jasmine came out. And God was she beautiful.

She wore a white dress that made her look even more elegant than normal. She had some heels that, I later joked about, made her a couple inches higher and just at my shoulder height. Her mom smiled and her dad just gave me a joking glare.

"Cat got your tongue Jason," Jasmine asked, or so I was told later. I wasn't sure what she had said, I was too busy staring at this goddess.

Mr Kibbler said "I want her back at five."

Jasmine glared daggers at the poor guy while Mrs Kibbler, thankfully, said "Ignore the pussycat. Bring her back after the dance Jason."

"Will do ma'am," I said as I walked over to Jasmine. I passed her the vase of asters, which brought out her mesmerising smile. She handed them to her mom to take care of, and turned just in time to see the corsage I got her.

The corsage was the same colour blue as my shirt, which matched her painted fingernails. After a few seconds of fumbling I pinned the corsage for her.

With that done, her mom took millions of photos of us as all moms seem to do. After the photos me and Jasmine walked to the car and began the drive to the dance. As I had planned the second song was *In Case You Didn't Know* instrumental. And so I sang the song word for word to Jasmine, who was probably happy when I stopped singing.

At the gardens we were greeted by some teachers who came to help with the dance. We striked our names off the list for the dance, and walked through to where the dances would be. The main pavilion had transformed since Me and Jasmine first visited the area.

The once plain room changed into a highly decorated one. There were tablecloths with both the sunset and garden theme on all of the tables that were originally there. A few extra fold up tables were decorated by a few artists to show a landscape of flowers shining in the sunset's last rays. There were tiny lamps that had a paper shade around it to adjust the lights color to make it glow like the sunset when it became dark. The stage area was covered in the DJ's equipment. One side of the pavilion had three tables filled with food and drinks for the party, all generously provided by Jacked Fries. The wooden floor was cleaned until it shined. There were also a lot more people, whom me and jasmine at least said hi to.

All in all, the place had a more enjoyable feel to it.

The DJ played a bunch of fast pitch songs that we danced to and sang along with. Everyone was having a good time, but of course, as with every school dance ever, there was some drama.

It started the moment Jasmine and Kira went to dance while I grabbed a drink. I was grabbing a cup of sweet tea, which, as any southerner would tell you, is the best drink. I had just finished pouring myself a cup when Kayla walked over.

People asked me later how I knew someone was coming, and I just said it was some sixth sense warning me. I looked up at her and cursed under my breath.

Kayla got really close, like three inches away close. "I didn't know you were on the menu," she practically purred.

I looked at her and said loud enough for those around us to hear, "I'm not. Though I didn't know you were too slow to realize what being rejected meant."

The nearest students covered a grin, some though weren't fast enough to hide it before Kayla saw it. "Well you won't reject me for long," Kayla said as she tried to press her body against me.

Now my back was against the drinks table, but that didn't stop me from avoiding her. I moved to the side, out of her way and she leaned right into the table. And her arm knocked my tea right on her dress.

"See when you're thirsty you're supposed to pour the drink in your mouth not on your dress, I said in a voice I'd use when scolding Olivia.

Now I'm not one to normally be a rude person, but I was getting tired of Kayla. She kept trying to ruin Jasmine's happiness, and in doing so she was getting me mad.

Though apparently all of the other students agreed with me. Most of them were laughing and the others were trying to suppress the fits of laughter.

"Now look here," Kayla started to say angrily.

I raised an eyebrow and said, "And If I don't what will happen? Will you send big bad Matt after me," she nodded. I laughed "He's no threat to me. So why don't you look here. You're ugly. And I'm not talking about the outside, though you definitely don't hold a candle to Jasmine. Your ugly on the inside. You enjoy seeing people bullied, and you love hurting others. I really didn't want to do this, especially not in front of all these people. You're not giving me a chance though. You keep coming after me trying to hurt the woman I love."

"Well I've had enough of that. If I have to tear you down over and over again so you'd leave Jasmine alone, I'd do it in a heartbeat." I gave her a sad smile and walked away.

And as I was walking I walked straight into Jasmine. She was sitting there smiling. Later I'd learn that Kira saw Kayla walk over here and told Jasmine.

"Even with those two extra inches I couldn't see you," I joked.

Jasmine feigned a frown and replied "For a moment there, I thought you were actually a sweet guy."

And With a simple hand signal, that looked like a wave with two fingers, the plan that me and the other guys had made went into motion. The DJ saw the motion, glanced at a neary clock and nodded his head. I led Jasmine near the end of the pavilion and waited for the current song to end.

And when it did, the song *Speechless* by Dan and Shay came on. I looked at Jasmine and offered her my hand. "May I have this dance m'lady," I asked her.

She nodded and we danced. Now considering I didn't check the time myself, I got the timing perfect. As the final words were sung the sun set.

A quick glance around the room showed that Kyle's picked song was next as he made the hand signal. *Slow Dance In A Parking Lot* by Jordan David began to play. And Again me and Jasmine danced, as did our group of friends.

Antwan's song came on next. It surprised all of us really. *Wanted* by Hunter Hayes was the song he picked. Though all of us finally understood why he picked it as a beautiful smile grew on Christie's face.

Bryce was the final one to pick a song, and he picked well. Lee Brice's *I Don't Dance* played as the final song before the last light of day was gone. He and Miley danced in the center of the pavilion, lost in each other's eyes.

And to my complete surprise, Drake raised his hand in the same signal as us. He walked over to Kira and asked her "May I have this dance?"

She grinned from ear to ear and said yes. *A thousand years* by Christina Perri (Yes the song on Twilight) started to play. And they danced to the surprise of all of us but Bryce.

When the song ended the music stopped as the summer court was announced. "The junior prince was Matt Dennington, but seeing as he couldn't come, Bryce Harper was his runner up," My mom said

Bryce walked up to the stage and smiled. We all cheered for him of course, which caused him to blush a little.

My mom congratulated him and then said "The junior princess is Kayla Smith."

There was a lot less cheering and a lot more puzzled looks. Nobody could remember voting for her. Which of course they hadn't. Kayla did the votes and rigged it so she would be princess.

The senior's got called out as well, but I wasn't paying attention. I was chatting quietly with Jasmine when I heard my mom say "Jason Wilson."

A roar of cheering and applause went around the room, but I was confused. "What just happened," I said to Jasmine.

"The summer king has been chosen, your majesty," she replied.

I stammered "I-I'm the king?"

"Yes. Now get up there," Jasmine said shoving me towards the stage.

I still couldn't believe I had become the king. Yeah my popularity had risen a lot since the scrimmage game, but to earn enough people's respect to be king? That's crazy.

All of that ran through my head as I walked onto the stage. As cool as it was to be king, I really didn't like all of the attention.

I bowed my head down so my mom could put the summer crown, which was a crown made from different flowers entwined together, on my head.

Since I couldn't chat to Jasmine now, and my mom was standing next to me, I heard her next statement. "The Summer queen is Jasmine Kibbler," she said.

If the cheers for me were loud, the ones for Jazmine were deafening. She walked towards the stage with a huge smile plastered on her face.

Unlike me, Jasmine didn't seem to have problems with being the center of attention. She waved to everyone then bowed her head so my mom could place her crown on it.

Once the cheers died down, my mom said "And without further adieu, it's time for the royal dance."

Each pair of princes and princesses grabbed each other's hands and walked to the dance floor. Of course I led Jasmine down to the dance floor with a smile on my face.

The speakers started to play a song that brought us "royal" dancers to a nice slow dance. Luke Combs, *Beautiful, Crazy* made a lovely song to dance to. Though in all honesty I would've danced with Jasmine to any song. I was lost in her eyes, which always seemed to be changing shades of color slightly.

I was so lost in the moment, in the dance, and in her eyes, that I didn't even realize the song had ended. I also didn't notice all of the other people, who seemed to have just appeared on the dance floor. What keyed me in on the dance being over was the sound of applause.

I blushed a little, or I hope it was only a little. That seemed to make the crowd of onlookers cheer even harder.

With many people asking for my hand to dance throughout the night, and me seeing if Jasmine was okay with it, I had a night full of dancing. Jasmine had her night filled with dancing too, but we somehow managed to dance together every few songs.

The dance slowly winded down to just the lunch bunch, including the newer members of the inner circle. As it turns out we were the ones who all decided to do the closing for the dance.

We all joked as we tore down all of the decorations we used for the night. It was a perfect moment to be filled with laughter and friendship.

Though my favorite moment happened after they all left. Me and Jasmine did one last sweep for trash, and then were going to meet up on the dance floor.

Being sneaky, I swept past my car and grabbed a bluetooth speaker. I set it up on the dance floor and when Jasmine got there I hit play on my phone.

An instrumental version of *In Case You Didn't Know* started to play. I offered my hand and Jasmine took it. And as we danced across the floor, I sang the lyrics to Jasmine.

The song ended and I was staring right into Jasmine's mischievous eyes. In the moment I didn't know that would be one of my favourite three moments in life. We stood there smiling at each other for minutes, then finally I kissed her.

To be continued

Authors Note

I'd like to thank my friends and family for supporting me through this as well as my teachers and librarians who gave me advice when I needed it. This book is totally made up from my own mind and if there are similarities in names or stories that's just by chance. I want to thank each and everyone of you for reading my book and I hope it brought you joy. I want to throw a really special thanks to my twin sister Alicia Bartlett for drawing the cover of this book.

I really enjoyed writing this book and hope that I'll be able to get the sequel out within a year but only time will tell.

And to all of you who enjoyed the story waiting for the second one, you will have to wait a little longer than you'd think. I'm currently working on a whole different book with a different series called the weaponsmasters which is more of and adventure like book than it is romantic. There is as always with my works going to be some romance in it.

Sincerely, JB

Bryan Bartlett